Be Careful What You Wish For

From the memoirs of Adele Ohanzee Bijour
and her struggle with Lupus

Adele Ohanzee Bijour

Be Careful What You Wish For: From the memoirs of Adele Ohanzee Bijour and her struggle with Lupus

ISBN: paperback   978-1-970135-14-5
      hardcover   978-1-970135-16-9
      eBook   978-1-970135-15-2

This is a work of fiction. All of the characters, names, incidents, organizations, and dialogue in this novel are either the products of the author's imagination or are used fictitiously.

Scripture quotations marked **NASB** are taken from the New American Standard Bible®, Copyright © 1960, 1962, 1963, 1968, 1971, 1972, 1973, 1975, 1977, 1995 by The Lockman Foundation. Used by permission.

Any people depicted in stock imagery provided by Thinkstock are models, and such images are being used for illustrative purposes only. Certain stock imagery @Thinkstock.

Published in the United States by Pen2Pad Ink Publishing.

CONTENTS

To Whom It May Concern,

Be careful what you ask for. This is my warning to you! Be prepared because you may indeed receive that request but it may come to you in a way that is totally unexpected and unwanted. There were two particular times of my life that I asked for something and my requests were granted.

My first request came after a failed revenge marriage that produced a daughter. I was a single parent for three or four years working, struggling to make ends meet and I was tired of it. I decided I didn't want to do it any longer. So, I asked God to please bring me a husband. Someone who would love me and take care of me. Well my God is a good God! He generously brought me a wonderful husband, but that husband was also a drunk and an incredible womanizer that really didn't like me much. I still kick myself for that request of God.

My second request was to stop working as a vice president of a rather large bank, drive a minivan, take my kids to and from wherever they needed to go, be a PTA mom and do volunteer work. I so wanted to be that stay-at-home mom who prepared meals and would be there for their children just like the ones I saw on television. Well that request was also granted. I was able to retire from my job, got a van, gave my kids a full-time mom and my husband a full-time wife. That blew up in my face big time!

The reason I was able to quit my job was because I was blessed with an illness. That wolf is called Systemic Lupus Erythematosus and my retirement was medical. The second request is the one I want to focus on because that is what brings me to sharing my journey with you. My hope is that someone can gain something from the struggle of Lupus. I hope people are able to understand that although it does not necessarily kill you, it pulls out all the stops to make your life miserable.

I lived a good portion of my life miserable because of what I asked for. The consequence when you ask for something without thought or preparation is similar to getting the Genie in a bottle and you get three wishes. Your wishes come out to be just the dumbest things you could ever imagine. For instance, you asked for $1 million dollars but never specifying how when or why and the Genie grants your wish, but that million dollars comes as monopoly money. That's why I say viii be careful what you ask for. In asking for these two things, I have led a pretty overwhelming life over the past 25 years. So, I have decided to share my journey and what it was like living in the situations I've asked for. Specifically, the Lupus rollercoaster... the highs and lows. I should admit, there were good times especially during my manic episodes. However, when you weigh the good times against the bad, the bad supersedes everything else because the good was predicated on my mental state.

I think about how I reacted and responded to the things that went on with my life and it leaves me somewhat embarrassed. I did some things in retaliation that will make you laugh, make you cry and make you want to choke me. In the end though, I knew that there was a purpose for everything I've gone through. It just took me most of my life to understand and accept that. Now, I'm living out the final chapters of my life. I am very grateful for what I've been through. I am respectful of the purpose that has been imposed upon me. This is my life of living with Lupus. The aches of getting through each day living with a disease that currently has no known cause or cure. This disease has caused me to feel trapped and like I couldn't survive the world. My purpose here is to relay how I turned my hardships into a loving peaceful life.

My battle of living with the cause and effects of such a devastating disease which I wouldn't wish upon my worst enemy. Come along on my journey of Lupus...

Luv's up,

Adele

Chapter 1

THE MASQUERADE OF THE PURPLE BUTTERFLY

Arlin and I got married April 14, 1995 on a beach in Michigan. I can still hear the echoes of the water splashing against the rocks on the shore as we exchanged our vows. That moment marked the beginning of a lifetime of memories we'd share together. I was raised in Victoria. My husband Arlin was raised in Minnesota. So, once we were married we decided to move to Lakeville, Minnesota. Together we had four children, two girls and two boys with four very different personalities. Our oldest was Adara. She was a challenge. Then there was our indifferent son Bennett. He was not bothered by much and a bit self-absorbed. Next, there was our sweet heart Abella. She was our quiet baby. The two of us had a special bond. Finally, there was our baby Bryce. I referred to him as "Mr. know it all." Not too much got by him.

Then there is me, Adele. I had always been a hard worker who demanded perfection, which left me disappointed most of the time. My heritage is a bit of a mix. I am French, African American and Native American. I love what my middle name means in my Native American culture. Ohanzee means that I am an intellectual wolf, thoughtful and enjoys solving interesting problems, with above normal intelligence. When down, this wolf gets back up as fast as possible, focuses on things that are important and shrugs off the less important things in life. That would be me!

Arlin is a smooth, cool operator. He is quite handsome, charming, and very reserved. He is a very curious and outgoing gent when it comes to women. It's safe to call my husband a womanizer. I present to you The Hamilton family.

Moving to Lakeville was an easy decision to make because we both had jobs there. The move seemed logical instead of continuing to make the hour and half long commute to and from every day. Shortly after the move I began noticing my husband was becoming more and more unhappy with his job as a United States Postal Carrier. He had been in this position for a few years but was beginning to toy with the idea of going back to school. Could it be the answer to the unsettled feelings he'd been having of wanting to do more with his life? He tried school only to quickly realize that wasn't it. Then he confided in me that more and more each day he had this growing urge to give back to his community. He applied for a position with the Minneapolis Police Department and was accepted.

All of a sudden, he was slapped with the reality that he was leaving a stable job to start over doing something where he thought he could help. It took time for things to set all the way in for him after the initial realization. However, I was totally on board! I was also very proud to be married to a man with such conviction.

Due to certain city ordinances, Minneapolis required all police officers to live within city limits. We uprooted and happily moved to Minneapolis, MN. We found a nice bungalow to rent and the schools for the kids were ok. They had no opposition to the move. They were happy that their dad was going to be a cop. Although the move shortened the distance we both had to travel in to work, I still had to commute to my job, which I was more than happy to do. This turned out to be a great opportunity for my husband and our family. Arlin progressed through the ranks over the years and eventually was promoted to Chief of Police for the city of Minneapolis.

Meanwhile, I was joyfully climbing the corporate ladder at the bank I worked for. I started as a part-time teller and proceeded to move through the ranks with hard work and determination. I was proud of my status and moving up to the position of Vice President was the ultimate joy. I did not mind the early morning or the late evening commutes because it gave me time to reflect and make plans for the next day. I didn't start thinking about my family until I got closer to home. I had to prepare myself for stories of the day and the demand for dinner.

After Arlin completed the academy and exceled during his

probationary stint, we decided it was time to look for a house. That was exhausting! We were hoping to find something at the edge of town. We had decided in advance that we would stay in a range that the mortgage could be afforded by one of us if something happened. That was hard because we saw quite a few that were in our approval range that had Adele's name on them. We settled on one. It was just lovely. It needed minor pre-move in work but it was nice. I loved my house.

I began to notice that the drive to and from work was getting more and more difficult. When I got home all I could see was my bed. The kids were often left to fend for themselves. If they wanted to talk or needed papers signed for school they had to meet me in bed. I felt so bad for them. I found myself rising very early in the morning just for quiet time and to get dinner going for the evening. Arlin was working the late shift so he was a big help in the beginning. He was so compassionate and never ever questioned me when I wasn't feeling well. I just couldn't put my finger on what was actually bothering me. I just felt tired. I was sure I was losing my mind. I was going to the doctor but all I could come up with was a virus. I was plagued by symptoms I could not put a name to except exhaustion. I had even started to drink coffee and anything else that could give me a little energy. The achy joints had me feeling like an old lady. The pain was everywhere in my body. Even breathing was getting hard. I kept asking if I had cancer. I got a definitive no on that but no other answers.

I was tested for thyroid issues and anemia. I did always have a fever and low white blood count. This "flu" persisted and landed me in the hospital on more than one occasion. However, I was always released to go home with a virus of some sort. I was seeing the same general practitioner as Arlin. He was intrigued with me mostly because he was an inner-city doctor and didn't see many, if any cases like mine. I am most grateful to him because he didn't treat me like it was all in my head. Many people I have come to know in my situation all say this is the worst part... doctors treating you like your nuts! Dr. Anderson was not giving up. He was determined to find out what was going on.

It's funny now as I think back, Arlin and I had applied for life insurance policies. Because of the amount, the company required a health screening and a urine sample. We were turned down for the insurance because I had protein in my urine which was a red flag that something serious was happening with my health. The insurance company said I needed to see a doctor right away. We didn't pursue it immediately but when I went back to see Dr. Anderson he did a urine test. It was still there but he was unsure why. No doubt my kidneys were becoming involved. This was the beginning of the unfortunate rest of my life.

The first diagnosis was Multiple Sclerosis. After that it was Vasculitis. Then they said it was Nephritis. The Nephritis was right. My kidneys were inflamed and lead to kidney disease. So, it was time to put everything together. I was anemic, had a low white blood count, positive antinuclear-antibody (ANA) test, kidney biopsy showed kidney disease, excessive protein, rapid weight loss, sore and achy joint pain, constant fever, sore throat, the magical butterfly rash across the bridge of my nose, the other miscellaneous rashes over my body, the fact that I couldn't stand to be cold, and lastly the constant headache.

Now the Lupus idea was starting to float around because of the rashes. A breakout on the face in that type of pattern usually meant Lupus. It's called the butterfly rash or the wolf. I was losing weight at the speed of lightening. I was upset that I couldn't enjoy the weight loss because I was too sick. Finally, another kidney biopsy was ordered and what do you know, I finally had a firm diagnosis. I'm wasn't crazy and I hadn't experienced the longest bout of the flu in history! After three doctor consultations, it was determined I had Systemic Lupus Erythematosus. What the What? I had never in my life heard of such a thing.

After nearly two years of feeling as if had the flu or a virus, I had finally been given the correct diagnosis. The road was long and tough! All my symptoms began after I had a hysterectomy for fibroids and endometriosis. Then a year later I had an Oophendectamy because the endometriosis was still present and causing problems. These two surgeries could have been responsible for the Lupus becoming present. It was said it was probably always in my system and when something traumatic happened to my body like surgery, it triggered the Lupus and brought it to the forefront.

Now what? My body was going downhill rather rapidly. Getting to work was so difficult. Once I made it I was so tired I couldn't function. I was glad I had the talent of delegation with no selfish fear of someone doing a better job than me. I was very precise in the work I would delegate out to my staff. Always matching the personality and talent to the task at hand. My actual illness was unknown by the general staff. They just knew I was ill. Of course, the rumor mill had me dying from AIDS because of my appearance. That little theory came from the group that didn't like me. I never addressed the rumor because I had never been one to give a rat's ass about what someone thought of me. Others thought I had cancer. Sometimes I wished it was cancer. My thought process was at least I would know what was coming.

Now it was time to research this thing they called Lupus. I spent many days researching Lupus trying to understand exactly what I was up against. I learned an abundance of information. The word Lupus itself refers to several forms of a disease of the immune system that affects joints, skin, kidneys and other parts of the body. It was also referred to as the wolf. People with Lupus have an overactive and misdirected immune system. What happens is your immune system acts as your body's natural offense against infections like bacteria and viruses. But, when you have Lupus, the immune system produces antibodies that react with the body's own tissues. That's why it's referred to as an autoimmune system disease. In most cases, the term Lupus refers to the form known as Systemic Lupus Erythematosus, or SLE for short.

According to the Arthritis Foundation's study on Lupus, it is an inflammatory condition that may be chronic. Inflammation refers to a reaction that results in pain, heat, redness and swelling. Chronic means the condition is long-lasting, which could mean it lasts for the rest of your life even though you may not experience symptoms on a constant basis. Many people with Lupus have changes in signs and symptoms known as flares and remissions. A flare is a when the disease becomes more active with increased symptoms. During a remission, few or no signs or symptoms of Lupus are present. Sometimes a person may have a complete or long-lasting remission, but this does not necessarily mean the disease has gone away.

I also learned from the Arthritis Foundation in my studying that the immune system does not function properly and produces antibodies called autoantibodies that react with and damage the body's cells, tissues and organs. This process is known as an autoimmune response. Auto means self. In Lupus, there are many different types of autoantibodies are formed, although the most common autoantibody is produced against the nucleus of cells, and therefore called anti-nuclear antibodies or ANA for short. There are several different types of ANA such as anti-double strained DNA or anti-Smith antibodies, which are unique to SLE. Anti-nuclear antibodies are found in almost all cases of this. Rheumatoid Arthritis and Sjogren's Syndrome are two common conditions that accompany Lupus. However, it can also be found in some healthy people.

About 90% of people with Lupus are women. In most cases, symptoms first appear in women of childbearing age 18 to 45. But Lupus also occurs in children and in older people. African Americans tend to get Lupus more often than Caucasians. Some studies suggest the disease may also occur more often in Asian and Hispanic populations than in Caucasians.

What I found was very scary and quite unnerving. It seemed that my case was extreme. I was certain I wouldn't live much longer. One of the first things to jump out was that no two people suffer the same way. Medication started ruling my life. The miracle drug and killer drug Prednisone became my companions for life. My dose was so high that the weight came back quicker than a blink of an eye, but I was feeling better. It gave me loads of energy but it turned me into a starving lunatic! There wasn't much I wouldn't eat. It was like I was pregnant. The cravings were unreal and strawberry cheesecake was my weakness. When Arlin cared and was working late he would bring me cheesecake from my favorite restaurant.

By this time, I was on one of many medical leaves. I was doing things around the house, cooking up a storm, taking the kids wherever they needed to go. I was a ball of crazy energy and often out of my mind. The different medications would bring out different personalities. Because I was gaining weight like crazy Arlin went out and purchased an entire new wardrobe for me, but I grew so fast I never got to wear one outfit.

I felt like I was on my own from the start. Arlin didn't go to doctor's appointments with me due to his schedule. Nor did he go to hospital procedures. He would pretend to listen as I filled him in on the latest findings when he wasn't really interested. I was no longer the youthful vibrant woman he married. Honestly, he lost interest before I got sick. The womanizing wasn't new. They were always a part of our marriage. The only thing different was now that I was sick, he had more free time to take on more affairs. I used to laugh when his females would find out about each other. To be honest, I don't know how he did it. One time I got a hold of his phone and three different women left messages for him saying they had made dinner for him and they would see him when he got there. I admit I hated hearing these other women talking to my husband, but what was I going to do? After all, despite a few flaws he was a good guy. Plus, I figured I didn't have long to live so to hell with it! Not that I was strong...it was just the opposite. I was too weak and sick to care.

My two oldest kids knew something was going on. I explained the best I could. Bennett was Bennett, just plain old indifferent. If it didn't concern him he was good. Adara was one that needed to know everything. She was researching, asking questions and looking after me. She was my rock. She was still a little pistol even when out of my presence. She picked up my slack directing traffic and deciding who could see me or call me. When I went to the hospital she always provided the EMTS with all the pertinent information. Adara was also my problem child and we clashed often. This made me even more proud of her because she stepped up. My two youngest children were just glad when mommy was home, especially when I was on medical leave. Home was where they thought I should be. I loved when Abella and Bryce would climb into bed with me and both of them would lay on me like a blanket. They had no idea how much pain they were causing but it was worth it. I needed to feel loved.

My mom and dad were very worried and crushed by this. They had no idea what this disease was nor did they care. They just wanted it gone. They couldn't accept the fact that their baby was sick. All they knew was that whatever this was it seemed to be killing their baby. My mom was trying to be supportive. She had some understanding about being sick because she had lived most of her life with various illnesses. I talked to her daily and gave her a rundown of my day. Some of Arlin's family members were supportive, though I think they were questioning my illness.

With the diagnosis finally in, all I could do was continually wonder what my destiny would be. At this point, all I could do was pray about it and ask for knowledge and strength. I wonder about my destiny even today and I am scared! I am worried about leaving my children here in this world alone. I also wondered if Arlin would in fact leave me because at this point I was useless. I was just worried.

Chapter 2

CALLING IT QUITS

At the beginning of this terrible disease all I could think about was the fact that I no longer wanted to live. I felt like I was useless to my family. I couldn't do my job very well and most of all I hated how I felt. My body was going through so many things that I couldn't figure out which one to focus on. I was terribly upset that I had a husband that was a cheater when I chose him. Yes, I said when I chose him! At the time, I thought he was the perfect guy. He was so loving, generous and attentive that I couldn't imagine he would have time for anyone else in his life. But Arlin proved me wrong time and time again.

The things I was experiencing with my body were things I could never imagine happening to one person at the same time. There was nothing good about Lupus. The medications I was on caused me to gain large amounts of weight. The one particular medicine that caused the weight gain was called prednisone. Aside from that, I lost my hair, had rashes all over my body, and had absolutely no energy! There were times when I couldn't walk up and down the stairs and was often confined to my bedroom. It always felt as if I had a never-ending flu. Those around me looked at me as if to say, "there's nothing wrong with you. Get up and do what you have to do."

On November 19, 1998, my life took another drastic turn. During a visit with Dr. Anderson, he told me it was pretty much over for me. My life was coming to an end! Pretty powerful words coming from Doc. His opinion was that I was going to continue to be driven down by Lupus. I never knew what was coming next but the funny thing was this actually happened on a good day. I wanted him to say it to me again. This was it. He did! My response was "but how can you play God?" He told me the facts of my case again and I should get my house in order. This was the first time of many that he or another doctor told me it was over.

I was only a couple of years in at this time. When I was diagnosed there was a ten-year life time on my head. I figured I could no longer live in this nightmare and the best way to get out of it was to die. My children were looking at me hoping that I would do something different this day but all I could do was stay in the bed. I was disappointed in myself. I thought long and hard about the process of suicide, about the people I would be leaving behind, about the legacy I would be leaving behind, and what life would be like without me here. I thought about each one of my kids, Adara, Bennett, Abella and my baby Bryce. I knew they would be disappointed but deep down within me I felt they would be grateful in the end because I was no longer here weighing them down. I could only hope that they would forgive me for this awful crime I was about to commit. I refer to it as a crime because to take one's life is just that... a crime. As for Arlin, all I thought about was how I could get back at him for everything he was doing to me while I was going through all this pain. Though I wanted him to feel the pain I was feeling I knew even if he did he would bounce back very quickly.

I researched all of my medications very well. The medication that could do the most damage if not regulated, was the prednisone. Prednisone works with your adrenal glands. What I found out was that if you take your prednisone in the morning your body knows not to produce your adrenal glands. So, I knew that if I played around with my prednisone I could get it to take me out. I will not go into the details of my plan for fear that it may give someone else the same idea, but what I will say is that I was not consistent with taking the prednisone. Then I would become consistent taking the prednisone, thus making my body confused and unsure of what it needed to make my body survive. Well it worked... kind of. I laid in the bed day after day waiting and waiting until my body could no longer handle the stress. After a few days, I was nearly incoherent.

My daughter Adara came in my room, as she often would, to sit with me for a while. I'd give her instructions on what needed to be done in the house, what bills needed to be paid, and other odds and ends. This particular day Adara said,

"Ma you don't look right. Should I call dad to come home?"
"No, not just yet."

Then for some reason the covers came off my legs and my legs were black. Now I'm a very light toned woman. Adara screamed!

"MOM what is wrong with your legs!" My response was quiet and calm.

"I don't know. What do you think?" She immediately called her brothers and sister up to the room and proceeded to show them my legs. It was funny because they were all examining my legs as if they were doctors, with the exception of Bennett. He just kind of stood in the background. He calmly said,

"I think we should call 911 but first I think we should call Grandma."

So Abella called her grandmother in Mississippi, but before Abella could speak Adara took the phone from her and yelled,

"GRANDMA! MOMS LEGS ARE ALL BLACK! WHAT SHOULD WE DO?" Judging by Adara's reaction her grandmother must've instructed her to examine the rest of my body.

Adara then told my mother "her entire body is black and she's not talking very much."

Adara quickly disconnected the call and called 911. After talking to the 911 operators, she called the district to have them send her father home right away. It was an emergency. All I could think of in that moment was that I was finally getting the attention I had been wanting all along and it's going to be the last time I get this attention. I looked at all of my kids with tears in my eyes, thinking that this is the last time I would see my babies.

I thought to myself *well Adele you gon' get your wish. This is happening. You don't turn this black for no reason.* My kids just sat around me on the bed waiting for the next step... whatever that may be. I wondered if I had waited long enough because I could still think and mumble a few words. I told each one of my kids that I loved them more than life itself. I started to have doubts. Maybe I didn't want to die but I didn't know if I had a chance to reverse this. As I was thinking these thoughts Arlin came running up the stairs. As he got to the top of the stairs and entered the room the rescue squad pulled up. Arlin yelled for the kids to move out of the way. He lifted me up and carried me down the stairs. As he got to the bottom of the stairs the squad had already rolled the bed in. Arlin gently laid me on the cart, kissed me on my forehead, told me he loved me and said he'd be right behind me in the squad car. That was the last thing I remember.

I awoke three days later a bit disappointed but happy just the same. The comments were all the same from the staff "You are one lucky young lady. We almost lost you." Then I remembered why I was there. I was there because I chose to be there! How selfish of me. My first rheumatologist who practiced at a different hospital came over to see me, which is not something doctors normally do when they don't have privileges at a hospital. He walked in with a disappointed look on his face. I was quite surprised to see him there. He looked at me, held my hand then said,

"You did this on purpose. You knew exactly what you were doing, right?" At first, I tried to lie but he stopped me and said,

"I know exactly what you did. If you ever try this again I will no longer be your rheumatologist. Is it a deal?"

"Yes Dr. Steve it's a deal." I replied.

I admit I was pushed up against the wall on more than one occasion but I never actually tried it again. However, I made plans for my demise on a number of occasions. This was the beginning of my therapy roller coaster. Do not, under any circumstances, be afraid to get help when the feelings of depression begin to overwhelm you. Various therapists I had saved my life a number of times. My therapists also saved the life of Arlin a number of times too! Psychologists, psychiatrists and therapists are all very strong assets to have in your arsenal of survival weapons.

Chapter 3

FIRST PANIC ATTACK

When I arrived back home from the hospital I was scared and miserable. Arlin was still supporting me and showing concern, which was comforting, and life picked back up as usual. I rested a few more days then picked back up with my daily routine and back to work I went. Yes, I was still working despite how increasingly difficult my days had become. The bank was beginning its move to the twentieth century and those changes scared me because I couldn't keep up. My mind was slowing down minute by minute. The one smart thing I did do was surround myself with all the smartest people under me. It appeared I was still getting the job done. I did not want to give up my job that I had worked so hard to get. The city of Lakeville had a taste of the first female black Vice President of loan operations. I took a lot of grief from some of our customers, but I also took lot of congratulations from many others.

My days were quite long when you add the thirty-minute commute. It started at five in the morning and I didn't get home until after seven. I usually worked early, before anyone arrived and after everyone left. It was the only time I could concentrate. My duties were extensive. I was sure they were testing my abilities. By the time I made it home I was dead. When I think back to those time I can't even remember what my children were doing or what they ate. All I remember is that no one complained. The boys were doing their sports things and working. Adara was busy looking for friends but she had more friends than we could count. She was the talking drum of the family. So much so that we had to have a second line installed for her gabby personality. Abella, my baby girl was just quiet doing whatever was needed. She seemed to have trouble with school but would never asked for help.

When it was my bedtime, Adara and Abella would always come to my room, put me to bed, and lay with me for a while. One would rub my feet and the other would rub my hands. I was in so much pain and I did not know how much longer I could keep going. Once they turned my light off and closed the door I'd just cry. How did I come so far and then have it taken away by this thing called Lupus? That night my prayer was simple and to the point

God... Dear God,

Please let me be a stay at home mom. I want to drive a minivan and be a PTA mom. Please Lord let me be a band mom. Let me be more involved with my children. Please don't let them raise themselves. My Lord, take me out of that job and let us still maintain our lifestyle. Lord, I am so sorry for such a selfish prayer.

When Arlin walked in I had to hurry and turn away. I didn't want him to see my tears. He knew... Arlin knew everything.

"What's wrong? How was work?" He asked.

"Babe I can't do it anymore."

"Don't worry about it. It will be okay" he reassured me.

"Some days are good but most days are bad. If I stayed at home I could do a better job at being a mother and wife."

"Can we still afford the house? We just got it?"

"Remember we decided on a house that we could afford on just one of our salaries."

"Ok whatever works is fine and you're fine and you will feel fine" Arlin said in his kind caring voice.

With a soft kiss, he closed his eyes. Now I have to figure this out. That's my job making things work. I awoke to sunshine beaming across my face. I am going in a little late today to take care of some business for the kids at their schools. As soon as I was done I was on the highway heading to Lakeville and The East Bank of Water Stone. That dreaded place of my employment. As soon as I walked through the door it was as if I had 100 kids wanting my attention. It was kind of like one of those television scenes where the main character says, "walk with me, talk to me."

When all their issues were dealt with I was then faced with my biggest problem... my new boss. He came in from another bank with our new president. His goal, it seemed, was to make every officer live up to their title. That scared me because I could no longer live up to mine. I had been out of the bank on a number of medical leaves. Each time I was gone they were pressuring me to return. How do I get out of here with grace?

The day went on as usual and with me faking my way. The Lupus had completely drained me. Sometimes I lived with a migraine headache. Often times I couldn't leave my desk because I was too dizzy. Sometimes I was so mean I scared people away with just a look. Other days I was in the bathroom throwing up all day. Then there were some days that I felt fine. The wolf, as they call it, was mean to me! I was feeling awful and not sure which way to turn.

I began drastically dropping weight and had lost so much weight people were starting to wonder what was up. That was the only fun part. I had to buy new clothes! One of my staff members came into my office and she said, "your clothes are falling off you. The suits you are wearing are about 10 sizes too big." I was so sick I hadn't noticed. My goal was to get to work each day. I was already depressed about this Lupus thing that no one was giving me answers for. When it became time to shop, that's when the manic-depressive disorder started to reveal itself. I was shopping every paycheck and no longer needing to buy from the big women's rack. I was able to buy off any rack. Now I was looking good. The Lupus was in full swing but my body didn't show it. I overheard employees commenting that I don't look sick. That is the worse statement one can make to a Lupus patient. "You Don't Look Sick" is a statement that could get you slapped!

Even though I was feeling awful I didn't want to leave early because that meant I had to inconvenience another officer to stay late to close the vault. I accomplished what I needed to do that day so I figured I would just stay put in my office at my desk pretending to be reading some of the new crap that was going to take place.

Well the day had come to a close. I was sitting, waiting to close the vault when suddenly my mind started to twirl. I can't do this today. I started to cry! First silently and then uncontrollably. Next thing you know I'm mumbling as if I needed to be wrapped in a white coat. I didn't know what was happening so I couldn't tell anyone else what was going on. Before I knew it I found myself hiding beneath my desk. I remembered someone asking if the rescue squad should be called or my husband. I yelled "NO, I'm fine just leave me alone!" That was my first panic attack.

As I began trying to settle myself down I started trying to figure out how I was going to get home to Minneapolis by myself. I wouldn't dare call Arlin because he always expected me to handle everything. So, I fixed my wig on my head (the Lupus took my hair out). Just as well I couldn't hold my hands up long enough to fix my hair. As I laid under my desk I thought to myself *I am good at this job. No one gave it to me. I worked for it. This damn Lupus! I'm not ready to give this up.* If I was going to keep it I would have to work 4 to 5 times harder to survive. I also thought about the big jar of candy I always had on my desk. I noticed that the jar of candy kind of signifies joy. Even when someone comes in angry or plans on telling me off my goal was to get that person to take a piece of candy when they left. As long as I focused on the joys of my job and the hard work I put in to get here I could conquer whatever this was and keep going.

With that thought I got up. Everyone had left, someone closed the vault, and it was time to go home. I got to my car and there was one of my favorite coworkers.

"Are you okay now? I've been waiting for you for a long time." He said.

"Get in. I'm taking you home." Robin said.

"I suppose you're going to come pick me up in the morning?" I asked.

"So, you're coming back?" he replied shockingly.

"Yep for the time being! I am driving myself home and I love you for waiting for me and offering to drive me home."

"Adele, you know I'm in love with you and I'll do anything for you."

"I know."

"I will see you in the morning."

I got in my car, still wondering what happened, and drove off. Though I was still a bit loopy I made it. At my turn off there was Robin waving bye. I wished Arlin acted like he cared.

For a change Arlin was home. He had even cooked dinner and all the kids were there too. They must've felt it was special for dad to be home cooking. They were not about to leave this. They were playing games and what not but briefly looked up to say hi. I dropped my brief case and jacket and headed toward the kitchen. Arlin was whistling and loading the dishwasher. He stopped to speak.

"Hi, how was your day?"

"Fine" I replied.

I noticed there was no plate for me so I grabbed a soda and headed for bed. I got to my room with tears in my eyes. Oh no! Not two panic attacks in one day! Take your meds and go to sleep. I said to myself *tomorrow is another day and I am going to do it.*

Chapter 4

MY LAST CHRISTMAS

Tomorrow came and went. As the days continued to roll by, I felt worse and worse each day but we were now approaching the holiday season. I realized this could be my last Christmas, so I decided I would do it up right! I wanted a big Christmas Eve party. That thought set the manic into motion. First, I insisted that we decorate the entire house in pretty blue lights outside and blue and red inside. We filled every window and all the bushes in the front and back of the house with lights. I put the white lighted reindeer in the front and the walkway was lined with white lights. It was so beautiful! Magical but not over the top. I had four trees fully and skillfully decorated. Decorating was one of my specialties. I could decorate a tree or anything for that matter. They all looked to be professionally done. Everything that could be decorated was, all while being very tasteful. Arlin was still supporting me and going along with whatever I said. He was all for the party because I guilted him with "this is going to be my last Christmas."

Now it was time to shop. We always had dollar limits for the kids, but none for us. That year Neiman Marcus was my favorite shopping hang out. I purchased everything from there, even my staff gifts which came with a high price tag. I made sure the gifts were wrapped by Neiman Marcus so they all knew where their gifts came from. I even selected a beautiful set of crystal candle holders for our new president. Then there was the family. I made sure everyone got good gifts. Now I must say Arlin knew none of this. I was on such a high. All he knew was that I was happy and occupied. The house was filled with gifts and the smells of the season.

In my job, I was also responsible for the informal Christmas party and the entire decorating for the bank, which was professionally done. So, for a manic with this much control there had to be trouble in the end. I wasn't giving the ending much thought.

Then came the Christmas Eve party which everyone was invited to. I must admit I didn't think they would all come, but they did. The menu was ridiculous. It was a whole lot of everything, even ribs from the famous little joint across town. I fixed ham, roast, mostaccioli, greens, black eyed peas, corn bread, dinner buns, shrimp, sweet potatoes, potato salad, even those chitter things. Yes! I said chitter things. Yuck! We also had all the deserts one could imagine. Nothing went together. There were three or four meals in this spread. Talk about manic crazy! I did it all by myself. I didn't ask anyone to bring anything. Still Arlin said nothing. I even had gifts for all the random kids.

Our tradition was to have a little church time, read Christmas stories, watch the movie A Christmas Story, and open gifts at midnight. By this time most of our guests were gone, so this tradition was pretty much our family, a few other family members and their girlfriends and boyfriends that didn't want to leave. When it came time to open gifts Arlin sat at the tree and handed out gifts one by one. Each person had to open a gift and show what it was. It was Christmas morning before we were done. I'd never had such a good time. Everyone was stretched out somewhere on the floor. The best part was we went to Arlin's mom's house for Christmas dinner, so we could sleep till noon.

As I started to come down from the manic high I hit rock bottom so hard I still have the bruises. After Christmas dinner the gift giving began. His mom was on a fixed income and rarely shopped for anyone, but this year Arlin's sister was living with her so I guess they decided to shop for everyone and I do mean everyone. The wives, girlfriends of the grands, nieces and nephews, even Arlin, got gifts. Everyone but me! That shade tree was in full bloom in the middle of winter in Minneapolis. I think all at once everyone realized it. I know my kids did. Adara was mad and everyone else was just quiet for a while. Then Mrs. Hamilton took me by the hand to her closet and showed me some things I could have. What on earth was in this woman's closet that I could possibly want? I was devastated. Arlin never spoke on it, but I did notice he threw his gift in the back of the closet never to be touched.

Just like that, the best Christmas ever was ruined! I knew my manic spree wouldn't end well. I left ahead of everyone else. There was a little manic left in me... angry manic. With that bit of energy all the Christmas decorations and anything resembling Christmas was gone except for the outdoor decorations. Everything was back in place including me. I was back in bed. My body shut down with my mood. When one is on a manic cycle the body makes the pain and discomfort obsolete. Now that the manic was gone, the depression took over along with a flare of Lupus.

I had taken the week between Christmas and the New Year off for vacation but I think I would have done better had I went to work. That entire week I rolled around in bed in so much pain my eyes even hurt. I felt like I had an awful case of the flu. I couldn't eat or drink anything. I had never been so hurt, but maybe I was just using that as a reason to be depressed. This was a new cycle for me. I was now contemplating suicide again. I couldn't stop thinking about how much I had done for everyone and I was hanging my feelings on this one thing. I finally called the doctor, and of course Dr. Anderson waved me right in. He took one look at me and called the hospital for a room for me. I had pneumonia.

Once I was admitted into the hospital it was determined I was also dehydrated and my white blood count was so low it was off the chart. My ANA tested positive that the Lupus was very active. While in the hospital I was thinking that this may have been my last Christmas. I was beginning to feel much better after they started pumping me with 120mg of steroids a day. Doc was a good guy. He made the actual diagnosis for Lupus. He took me off work three months and after hearing about my Christmas escapade, he also demanded I see a therapist.

He proceeded to make an appointment with her then gave her my background information. She was able to make arrangements to see me before I left the hospital. I was shocked that he was so serious about this. He told me point blank I had a lot of issues that needed to be dealt with sooner rather than later. Her name was Carlita Bell. Doctor Anderson said I would be released after my session with her if she thought I was safe. Well, needless to say that wasn't my last Christmas. Twenty-five years later I am still here fighting.

Chapter 5

TIME TO LET GO

Eventually I was released from the hospital and allowed to return back to work. I wasn't eager to get back because of all the changes that had taken place but I was ready none the less. I awoke bright and early so I could get to work before everyone else and get started. I knew it was going to take me longer than usual to get things done. Not too long after my arrival we were called into a staff meeting. It was announced that Mr. Fisher was going to retire and the bank was being bought out by one of the largest banks in the world. My mind instantly began racing and the decision to retire was made in that moment. I knew I could not compete and I couldn't bear the thought of being let go or demoted because I could not keep up with the changing times and technology.

I was going to miss Mr. Fisher. He was our previous president and was old school. All he wanted was for you do your job, use common sense and be fair. I loved that man. Mr. Fisher had been responsible for all of my growth. He was not big on titles or degrees. He taught me so much. It was rumored that he may be retiring soon because his health had begun to decline. I told my mom when Mr. Fisher left I was going with him. He was so special to me. When my father passed he was at the funeral. We had gotten very close. So close that the staff was wondered if we had something going on because I spent so much time in his office.

The reality of it was he and my father had the same kind of cancer but my father's was further along than his was. He tracked him trying to get a handle on what he had to look forward to. I gave him daily updates in addition to the goings on in the bank. He was very hands on. He even noticed when employees made large deposits to their accounts. One of my promotions came when a teller deposited a $300,000.00 check into her account. He called me in to inquire.

"Adele... I noticed a rather large deposit was placed into an employee's account. Where on earth did they get $300,000.00 from?"

"Her grandparents purchased a house for them."

"Well who are the grandparents?"

"Mr. and Mrs. Hampton. They own a rather large company in town."

"So, you know them well! Can you get a meeting with them and our top commercial lender?"

I opened the door and we got the business account. That's how Mr. Fisher worked. Sadly enough, that would also be the last big account I ever secured.

Soon after that Mr. Fisher retired and we got a new young president who had a lot to prove to the higher ups. We had an officers meeting to discuss the new president's plans and what he had observed since his arrival. I sat quietly with no more fight left in me. I had always been known as the spunky one that would give you a run for your money. Now I had shrunken to a very petite nervous lady. I didn't even recognize myself. Lucky for me this guy liked me and he knew the disability and sick leave rules. So, I wasn't high on his target list.

I guess my body was overwhelmed by all the changes because it forced me into another medical leave. It was then that I decided not to return. After twenty-five years of giving everything I had it was time to officially leave my position at the bank. The Lupus had won this fight. I felt so guilty because I was missing so much work. My position was not a position you could just hand over to someone and simply say "do Adele's job while she's out." While my main title was vice president of lending, I had at least 10 other operational duties on my plate. In my absence, was when they realized just how much I was responsible for. I handled everything with ease because I had something to prove to the business community as well as the banks big wigs. That was until the Lupus blew the lid off of everything I worked so hard to accomplish.

While on my final leave of absence I started feeling better and enjoying my new home and all the things that went along with it. I got my van that I so desperately wished for. I was my kids chauffeur and I was helping anyone that needed help cooking great meals and entertaining for holidays. Friends and family were wondering if I were in fact really sick. I was even getting daily calls from work trying to help staff out that had reluctantly taken over my responsibilities. Every conversation ended with "when are you coming back?" I even dug up a portion of the front lawn and put in new sod. The reason for all this energy? The all mighty miracle drug prednisone. With 80 milligrams per day I was jumping out of my skin with energy and hunger.

Then the depression set in big time. That was mainly because I still did not know what was happening to my body, especially with the weight gain. Then there was Arlin continuing on in his womanizing mode that was most depressing. Mostly because I knew but didn't try very hard to put an end to it because I knew I couldn't. I was so jealous of his women and I knew I could not compete. I was in therapy weekly but it was hard to work anything out because there was so much going on. During one session, my therapist asked me if I planned on going back to work. My response was "I don't want to". Dr. Carlita was a pistol and would not hold back on her thoughts. She said "figure out what you're going to do about your health or what it's going to do about you. Talk to Dr. Anderson and your specialist and try and get a handle on what you and your body could handle. From there the other decisions will start lining up. It won't be a quick process."

I did just that! I met with my doctor and he told me my body was in trouble and I should face the fact that I may not return to my present job doing the same duties as I had when I left. Maybe something part time in the future, but at that moment he was recommending fulltime disability. He asked if we could afford it being that we purchased our house a short time ago. I told him when we purchased the house we based our purchase price and mortgage on one salary in case one of us got sick or we split up.

I got my story together along with the facts involving me taking a medical retirement and going on social security disability then got an appointment with Arlin to talk. He was a weird character and a difficult man to catch up with. I ran the plan by him, including the fact that I would be a fulltime wife and mother devoting myself to him and the kids. I thought it would make his life easier so he could do his job without worrying about home. I would do everything. In my mind, I thought I might finally get to play the June Clever role that I wished for. Mr. Arlin Hamilton responded to me with "If you can make it work, its fine by me." With his blessing, I made an appointment with the bank president, Dan Ostrowski.

When working, my power suit was always black. But, the day of the appointment my power suit was bright red! Right down to the red super high heeled boots to match! With my letter of resignation in hand I headed to the bank. Yes, everyone saw me but I acknowledged no one. I was scared I might change my mind. He greeted me before I reached his secretary with a strong handshake. I didn't tell him why I requested the meeting though somehow, I was sure he knew. I decided to play the victim in this, using the Lupus for all I could get out of it. I began with a little small talk which wasn't my strong point. Then I got right to it. I told him how much I missed my job and coworkers, lying through my teeth, but I did resent the daily phone calls. The calls were not to check on me but simply to ask a question about getting something done. It put great stress on me and stress caused the Lupus to flare. I explained that it was a disease that was hard for me to begin a healing process with or be accepting of because it had no cure.

Mr. Ostrowski was not one of my favorite people though he was a very nice caring person. He struck me as a bit sneaky because he was young in such a big job. His sole purpose was to please the big wigs so I was always careful what I said to him. During our meeting, he was sympathetic to my situation but didn't say much. He said he would expedite my paperwork and wished me luck. That was that! Although when I got back into the van I figured out that I had pushed myself out of a retirement party and a good going away gift!

God had given me my wish! I got my van, my house, Beaver and the other kids were happy and Arlin was taken care of. Well, at least to the best of my ability. Everything I wished for was now a reality along with the monster they call Lupus!

BE CAREFUL WHAT YOU WISH FOR...

Chapter 6

ACCEPTING REALITY

It was a good day for a change. I was up and in the home office taking care of some business. I have always been the biggest procrastinator so I was feeling extremely proud. I returned messages, filled out forms, wrote letters, did all the things pertaining to the family and things I had promised others I would do for them. The family thought that because I was a banker I could solve any problem they might have. I loved my office. It gave me a sense of purpose and I felt like I was someone. That was something I missed after leaving the bank.

As I was sitting tall at my big oak desk working on the computer, the phone rang. I found myself answering

"Adele Hamilton speaking... how may I help you?" I laughed when I realize what I had done. The cheerful lady on the other end of the line socked me right in the stomach through the telephone line. "Hi there! This is Mary Davis from the Minnesota Police Human Relations Department."

"Hello back!" I cheerfully said, not having a clue what was coming next.

"Congratulations on your new baby boy!" She spoke excitedly. After a long pause, I began to laugh hysterically.

"Are you alright?"

"No... not really! I had my tubes tied after my last child, so if I did just have a baby someone owes me some money!" She started to stutter.

"You inquired about getting the new baby on Arlin Hamilton's insurance." Now I decided to mess with her a little bit.

"Do you mean Arlin wanted to add his new baby to his insurance?"

"No, it was you that called and left the message with my staff of all the details."

"So, when did I have this baby?" Now she was embarrassed because she knew she had messed up.

"No, I really did not have a baby and it was perhaps one of Arlin Hamilton's other women. He has a few, so I can't direct you to the right one, so you probably need to contact Mr. Hamilton directly."

I know her face was redder than a ripe tomato. Finally, she said,

"I'm so sorry for your troubles" then hung up.

Whew... what a blow! For years I had tried to talk Arlin into having a vasectomy. My nightmare was him having a kid outside the marriage. I was dealing with the infidelities but an outside kid... how would I handle that situation? Arlin and I had the talk on a number of occasions. He even went so far as to make an appointment a couple of times. I guess he couldn't bring himself to do it. He had different plans for his future and I most likely wasn't apart of them.

I sat there stunned but not all that surprised that one of his female tramps would hook him. Arlin was a good catch in the eyes of all the younger girls he came in contact with. Both in his job and at the bars. He was still young in his mind and not ready to give up the party. Nevertheless, I must make it clear... Arlin did not become a cheater because my having Lupus was too much for him to handle. I found him to be unfaithful early in our marriage when we were still living in Lakeville, before he joined the police department.

I wasn't interested in leaving him at that time. I had bigger plans for us and the older kids were young. I wasn't about to go back home to my parents again. After my first failed marriage, I took refuge with them and I wasn't doing it again. Arlin was very sociable. He played in all the basketball and baseball leagues he could. It wasn't the games that attracted him, it was going to the bars after that excited him. I remember going to his games and sitting alone watching different groups of females watch me. It was easy to know which groups were there for Arlin but hard to pinpoint which girl was the girl.

I caught him cheating so many times it wasn't funny. I often followed him, stalked him and would stake out his latest conquest. I did this to myself because he could come up with some good lies and I had to know the truth. Often, I would get home just before he would. The hood of my car would still be warm. I would confront him and after his untruth I would clarify my position on how I knew different. Then I would let it go. I just didn't want him thinking I was that stupid. One time he had the nerve to charge a hotel room on our card and even left the receipt in his pants pocket. His reason was hilarious! He got the room for his cousin... I just shook my head.

When we moved into our first home in Lakeville, I worked out a great deal with one of my regular customers to rent the house for a year. After the year we had first option to buy. We weren't sure we wanted to stay in the city so the offer was good for us. Unfortunately, the house was on a busy street so often I would glance out the window to see a female sitting across the street stalking Arlin. One night I decided to go out on an Arlin hunt! When I went on these hunts, I left the kids home alone. When I got pumped up I didn't think. This night, in particular, I found the car and brilliant me decided to steal the car! I drove his car two blocks away and came back for mine. I did this all the way to the house! I never knew how he got home and he never asked how his car got to the house.

One more good one then I'll move on. One day my Arlin came in and said he needed to tell me something. That something was diseases of the sexual nature! Oh, he cried and promised he would never cheat again. The most humiliating part though was going to the doctor and the health department. Obviously, I still didn't leave him. I always thought I needed him and I didn't want to fail at my already failed marriage.

Anyway, getting back to the phone call from the dreadful Police Department calling to ask me about the baby I had. I waited impatiently for Arlin to get in. When I approached him on it, his response was very cool. The older he got, the cooler he became. I suspect the Human Resource department had gotten in touch with him judging by his reaction. He said yes that person had a baby "but, but, but, it's not mine!" I was waiting for a better story. He said he went to the hospital to see the baby and it was clear it was white or something else, but it was definitely not black and not his.

So now it's time for the paternity test. The female had a choice of waiting for a state test that would take a few months for results or do it privately for a few hundred dollars. Well, I wanted an answer right away so, my little stash of money that I put away for the Timberwolf floor seat tickets had to go for the stupid test. I was pissed! The basketball games were my escape from my crazy world. So, I even demanded that I go with him for the test, but he wouldn't give on that one. I waited patiently for the letter. When the letter arrived, I was relived as I read, as Maury would say "YOU ARE NOT THE FATHER" but disturbed because he was still with this girl. The reality was that Arlin had fallen in love with a whore and a stripper! The funny thing was there was a song out at the time entitled I fell in love with a stripper. Every opportunity I got I made sure it was playing when Arlin was around. That was when he started hating me.

Still battling my health through all this, I tried to block out the drama of my life long enough to get through my next doctor's appointment. Doc was very familiar with Arlin's family. He had treated many of them. As we discussed my health he offered me a piece of advice. "Get rid of Arlin!" His cheating ways were taking a serious toll on me in the form of stress. He knew all about him from many reliable sources. He said, "remember I treat a lot of cops."

Okay then, which reality do I face? I am not giving up on my body, although I do admit suicide had been hanging over my head. I shared this with Doc and he immediately referred me to a wonderful doctor of Psychology. With that said, I think my reality was dealing with a husband that was in general a wonderful man with a major flaw. He was a good dad, a good police officer and most importantly he turned his paycheck over to me. My faults were as bad as his. He loved women and I loved to spend money. In some ways we were even.

By now I was diagnosed as a depressive/bi-polar manic. I was always depressed mostly because I wasn't the women I used to be and I couldn't keep my man to myself. Trying to keep the front of happiness going was a tough job. Arlin and I made a good couple. We always looked good and went to all the shows, plays and concerts together. We had a standing Saturday date night. The major problem I had with that was when we got home he always had to make a run so our dates would end with me going to bed alone. Although, I must be honest. I didn't really mind it all that much. By the time we got home I was in so much pain I just wanted to go to sleep. The next day was a new day. It was time to get my shop on and on more than one occasion I spent the mortgage money during one of my manic sprees.

I do believe I accepted my reality. Two wrongs don't make a right, but one can wash out the other. I lived with my father's infidelities. I remember when my father wanted to divorce my mom. By then she was indifferent. He went on his merry way until it was clear just how much he would have to give up. One day he walked through the door and said, "I'm home and I ain't leaving. This is my house!"

My mother walked past him and said, "No one told you to leave." They lived in that house together because my father found out it was cheaper to keep her and my mother found out living on a budget wasn't any fun. My mother knew all about Arlin. It seemed everyone did. I asked her what I should do. Her response was "you have to decide if it is worth it to stay or if you can make it without him." She added "you have to be able to be graceful and ignore the talk on the street." My mother was always graceful, as long as none of my father's women approached her.

There was this one time my mom found out that my father's girlfriend had put a hit out on my life. Her brothers were no joke. They were the scariest bunch in the city of Victoria. A few murders were of their doing. Nobody messes with Miss Adara's baby girl.

She found out that Nett, who was my father's girlfriend, and her brothers were up the road at this little bar. My mother was a

Jehovah's' Witness on most days of her life except that night. The woman I called mama stormed out of the house yelling at me to stay there. The story unfolded quite nicely. She pulled the car up to the bar, left it running with the door opened and proceeded to the trunk to grab the tire iron. She walked in, snatched Nett's wig off as she spun her around and proceeded to beat the living daylights out of her as her brothers watched! Mom turned toward the three gangster brothers and said, "Don't mess with my baby! I have never done anything to any of you nor has Adele and I am going to need you to respect that! Do I make myself clear?" All heads nodded in agreement.

The crowd parted, she got in her car, came home, grabbed a Pepsi and went to bed! I was the talk of the town for a long time. My mom was so cool and graceful she even became friends with the bunch! I knew the story in detail and why that woman's brothers did nothing. It was because my big brother and his friends were sitting in the back of the bar with a gun on the table, one in his waistband and one in his hand with his friends all packing. My brother didn't play either!

Yes, I had acknowledged my realities. I suffered from a very serious fight with Lupus, never knowing what was to come. My ailments ranged from kidney disease, thyroid disease, severe depression, constant headaches to manic depression. Little did I know there was a lot more to come. Another reality was that I did not want to let my husband go. I chose to remain hopeful that something would change, though being fully aware this was how it was going to be. I would never work again... that's a tough reality and I'd be depending on others. Now that I had accepted those painful realities which were long overdue, it was time for my search for God to begin.

Chapter 7

THE GUN AND ME

One day, Arlin slipped up. This was a slipup that could have ended both of our lives. He was always being very private with his belongings. He carried a bag with a change of clothes and what nots in the trunk of the car, but this time he left his bag in the basement's workout area. So of course, I took the opportunity to go through his belongings as I do on a regular basis. Well low and behold what do I find? A very beautiful and expensive looking ring that had the air of a wedding band. The ring had a pure look of love written all through it. It was a combination of silver and gold entwined together to hold two magnificent diamonds. The ring was something that I could have envisioned myself giving to Arlin. I had presented him with a few bands, but he always somehow lost them. So, I gave up on my husband acknowledging our marriage by wearing a band, though he knew how much I loved the sight of a married man wearing his wedding band. To me that was the ultimate turn-on.

The house was looming with my down trodden solitude, yet the smell of freshly baked Italian bread accompanied my masterful mostaccioli and Italian green beans. One would believe this was going to be a great family sit down dinner. I knew better, but the charade had to be kept intact for the kid's sakes. This particular day, Arlin came straight home from work, which he normally did not do. He must've had a hard day because he placed his gun bag on the stairs and went to the guest bath room. I'm guessing he couldn't make it upstairs. I was sitting at the dining room table trying to figure out how I would approach the subject, as I twirled the ring around my finger.

Normally when I caught Arlin in one of his female games, I sat on the newest heartbreak for a while to think of how I would approach him and his latest misstep. I would then decide if it was a losing battle that was worth my stress. More often than not I said nothing because it was nothing I could do about it. The Lupus left me at his mercy. Being sick and unable to work left me feeling pretty much confined to the situation. But, this was one of those times I just couldn't let it pass me by. I kind of had enough!

I got up from the table and headed to the guest bathroom where Arlin was sitting of the toilet taking care of his business. To get there I had to pass the stairs. Something in me snapped! I unzipped that beautiful leather gun bag that I had purchased for him during one of my manic shopping sprees at Niemen Marcus and gently removed his off duty white pearl handle 45 caliber handgun. It matched perfectly with his pearl while Cadillac SUV. As I took hold of it I caught a glimpse of my face in the shiny gun metal. I could see a tear glistening. I wondered if that tear was going to turn into a manic filled work of regret. As I turned and caught a full image of my face in the large gold framed entry hall mirror, I realized that lone tear was actually trying to put out the rage of fire in my eyes. Sadly, it was no match for the anger that fueled the gas in my body that was about to explode. I could hear the fuse closing in preparing for the biggest boom of my life.

I made sure the gun was loaded. With a sigh, I headed to the guest bathroom with the ring on one finger in one hand and the gun in the other hand behind my back. I kicked the door open! There he sat calm, cool and collected. Never uttering a word he just stared at me. I shoved the ring in his face screaming "Arlin Hamilton, what the fuck is this? Where did it come from? Who gave it to you? Do you have another marriage that I don't know about?" I wasn't hurt... just angry. I asked him again "where did the ring come from?" His response was "Just a friend. It's nobody... it's nothing... it's not a big deal." I was mad! I could feel the smoke billowing from my ears because the fire in my eyes couldn't be contained. From behind my back the .45 came out. I pointed it directly at his head. I wanted to shoot him between the eyes.

Suddenly, I could feel my body of emotions begin to change from madness and anger to hurt and heartbreak. I could feel the sweat dripping from my face as if I was fighting with my Lupus for my life, not fighting for his. It felt like hours were passing by with the two of us alone in this large but quiet house. In actuality, it had only been a few minutes. As I stood there pointing the gun at Arlin's face he finally spoke. His words did not surprise me, given his character. He looked me straight in the eye and asked, "do you want to shoot me?" I didn't answer. I just stared at him. He spoke again "go ahead and shoot me, do it if that's what you want!"

At that moment, the sweat that was dripping from my face was gone. The anger was gone but it left the hurt behind leaving me in knots. That was the moment another reality kicked in for me... the Lupus controlled my life. I was trying to kill the wrong thing! I could only be mad at me and the Lupus. Without the Lupus, I would have gotten rid of Arlin Hamilton long ago. I threw the ring at him. "You sorry-ass-son-of-a-bitch! Your life is not worth my life and I'll be damned if I'm going to go to prison and wear an orange jumpsuit for taking your ass out! Karma's a bitch!" I laid the gun on the counter beside him, walked away and headed up the stairs.

I didn't know whether or not he would pick it up and shoot me. I didn't know what his plan would be, but I had an idea. Nevertheless, it didn't matter to me at that point. What did transpire though is what was kind of amazing. He finished his business on toilet which I'm guessing he probably did when I pointed the gun at him. Cool Mr. Arlin went to the stairs, put his gun in the bag and walked out the back door. I watched him from the landing window. One would think that after what we had just experienced, his shoulders would have drooped with a bit of relief. But my sweet Arlin walked with the same amount of pride he had always displayed as a cop.

He even stopped to chat with the neighbors and plan a get together, all while playing with the dogs. Only he and I knew what had just occurred in our house. That was the moment I gave in completely. That night he came in at his usual time... about three or four a.m. He was good about coming home to wake up in our bed. I guessed it was to try and throw the kids off. I was still awake when he came in. As usual, I turned his side of the bed down rolled over and went to sleep. That day was never spoken of again.

This was our most volatile encounter. My payback or karma over the incident manifested almost immediately. The stress of the situation sent me into a Lupus flare, leaving me unable to function for nearly a week. Arlin did not suffer. Only I did. I had to figure out a way to live in this situation while keeping stress to a minimum.

The one thing I found amusing about this encounter was the prison statement of me not wanting to wear an orange jumpsuit. I never wore the jumpsuit, but my favorite color has been orange ever since.

Chapter 8

MALL OF AMERICA

I woke the next morning to find Arlin didn't make it home last night. Sometimes he overslept at one of his lady friend's houses. I just laid there trying desperately not to feel anything, but no matter how I tried I still felt the pain. Suddenly the house alarm went off. I could hear Arlin cussing under his breath. It always pissed him off when I set the alarm. This was how I would know when he got in. Since he was just getting in he was now running late. When he burst into to room I greeted him and asked, "What happened? Where were you?" His responses were always funny. "Last night I fell asleep on Tommie's couch". As usual, his uniform and gear were all in their proper places. He showered, dressed and kissed me on the cheek and told me he had a meeting with the mayor today.

Today was a day of doctors' appointments. I always felt so lonely and it was as if I was in this Lupus thing all by myself. When I first got sick Arlin was always with me. It gave me the illusion that he would be there for me, but that got old not long after my diagnosis. He never asked about my appointments so he didn't know much except what he could see... me always sick, never wanting to do anything, being lazy. The news today wasn't great. The Lupus was in a serious flare according to my bloodwork. Although I didn't feel that bad I knew it was coming. I wondered what part of my body was going to be attacked this time.

I decided to sit in the hospital lobby for a while before heading home. There was this nice looking older guy sitting across from me. I knew he was looking at me. He was waiting to make eye contact and finally our eyes met. He said,

"My sister, you look so sad and unhappy. I would make everything better for you if I could because you are too pretty to look so unhappy." I smiled

"Thank you... just your words have made a difference." With a big smile, I said, "Have a lovely day." I made my way to the parking garage.

As I reached my van my mood suddenly changed. Arlin's night out and that strangers' words gave me a burst of energy. That kind of energy meant the manic side of my bi-polar had kicked in and that was dangerous for our household. Arlin never questioned me about the money I spent as long as he got his allowance off top. What a dumb ass! I guess that's his guilt payoff. Rather than going home pretending to be June Clever and make dinner when no one's going to be there, not even the Beaver, I decided to take a trip over to the mall of America. That is one big mall! I was shopping for nothing in particular which is what was always so odd about these shopping sprees. I always bought Arlin something first, then I would buy everyone else something. I didn't just shop for myself.

When I go into my bipolar moments, either my depression had me down in the bed in a hole contemplating suicide or I was on a high. My high of course was shopping. This was one of ugliest faces of Lupus, I got hit twice. Lupus caused depression and the medicine they gave me caused depression and suicidal tendencies. As I strolled into the mall I smiled. It was time to shop! Money didn't matter, even if the bills didn't get paid. Everyone trusted I was doing right by my household, making sure everything was taken care of and it was a reasonable expectation, considering I was a Bank Vice President of Finance.

Shopping was the only time I felt like someone. Conversations with salespeople was the highlight! I had someone to talk to. While walking the mall all alone, before I entered my first store it was evident that I was one of the most unhappy persons in the world. I caught a glimpse of myself in the store window of Nordstrom's, one of my favorite stores. I looked so sad I wanted to hug myself. What a sight. My knees got weak and I had to sit for a moment before beginning my stupid journey. I normally would have to find a seat because my knees were so weak and my body was constantly fighting the Lupus. My normal was living like I had a bad case of the flu all the time. So, a pre-shop rest was normal.

I loved music. I got that from my mom. That woman was a devout Jehovah's Witness, but nothing was going to take away her love of music. Just like her we loved every kind of genre and I stayed up to date simply because of the kids. For them rap was in the forefront. I had certain songs I liked because I loved the heavy beats. I paid little attention to the lyrics, but I still banned the adult content in my house or my presence. Of course, the kids still got a hold of what they wanted. I admit I'm a Tupac fan, but a new hottie from the Midwest had hit the scene. I loved me some Arc. He was so fine and young and I had to have something or someone to fantasize about. We bumped him and the crew every time we got in the van. My kids and their friends thought I was cool. The fact is I was wishing I was living in another life.

As I sat on this long plush bench staring at the floor, I looked up to a young group of people enjoying themselves, loud and boisterous. As the group moved along, one of them took a seat at the other end of the bench. Someone yelled, "Arc aren't you coming?" My attention was now on high alert. I slowly looked down the orange velvet deeply padded bench and looked at this young man to be sure I was sharing the bench with my imaginary heart throb. Yep it was him! I knew I had to be cool even though I wanted to jump up and down screaming his name. Our eyes connected he said,

"Hello"

"You know I'm lovin' your cut. It's nice to have a new sound on the scene." I replied. He laughed at me

"What do you know about that?" He asked with a wink,

"Just because I've got kids your age doesn't mean I don't have something going on!" We laughed. He moved to my end of the bench.

"You don't know about me" he said with a sly grin.

"Here is my ticket to where my van is parked and I'll give you the keys. You'll quickly hear yourself." We laughed and that laughter never felt so good.

"I noticed you don't have any bags, what's up with coming to Mall of America and not shopping?"

"That was exactly my purpose but once here I didn't much feel like it."

"I know a beautiful lady like you can find a lot of stuff in big ass mall." Then he paused and leaned back and stared at me for what seemed to be and eternity. This boy was making me blush!

"What makes you so unhappy?" He asked

"What makes you think I am unhappy?"

"My grandmother used to tell me I had an extra sense about things."

"Well your granny was right. Yes, I'm somewhat of an unhappy soul, but it's nothing I can't live with. One thing I do know for sure... you have given me some happiness today and that's what I'm going to focus on right now."

In my mind, I was thinking maybe my mania would be used in a different way this time. I had been teased about being a cougar, often having to put my son's friends back in their age group. I am up for whatever right now. Just then his crew/entourage resurfaced. I was disappointed because Arc seemed like an old soul who could carry on a conversation that I didn't want to end. They smiled at me, being careful not to swear in my presence. I thought that was funny because I can out cuss a drunken sailor, though I appreciated their respect.

The discussion revolved around eating and PF Chang's won. Then they were going to chill at the hotel for the night. Their next show was tomorrow so they were free and pumped because the hotel they were staying at was in the mall as well as a night club. It sounded like such a fun life compared to my misery. *Just let me escape one time* was the song in my heart. After plans were made, suddenly Arc said "Y'all do what you do... I'll catchup to you all later." Everyone looked at me. Was I embarrassed? Hell no! I just smiled.

After the crowd was gone, he looked at me.

"My name is Carter and you are?"

"Adele... nice to meet you. Where did the name Arc come from?"

"A stage name my manager gave me and now that's pretty much the name I go by. We have been sitting here for a long time. You feel like moving around like to shop, eat or just walk?" I was in shock that he wanted to spend time with me. I love it though I was a bit fearful that it would turn bad. But, it couldn't be much worse than the life of loneliness and illness I was living. I was glad I dressed younger than my age that day. I looked pretty hot! So, I said,

"Let's walk and if I find something I want you can buy it for me."

We shook hands and agreed it's a deal. My confidence was off the chain now. We walked and talked for miles in that huge mall. Carter noticed I was slowing down and not talking as much.

"Are you okay or did I say something wrong?" He asked. The sincerity on his face melted my heart.

"No, it's me"

"So, you are sick! I saw you earlier in the mall and you looked sad like something was wrong and I was drawn to you." I figured he was being honest because what kind of game could he be trying to run on me. Lord knows I didn't have anything he would want. Finally, he said,

"How about dinner, what do you like?"

"I love PF Changs but not today" he laughed.

Chapter 9

THE ADVENTURES CONTINUE

We did have something major in common. My mother was French and his mother was half French. He had a little accent that I couldn't pick up until he told me his heritage. My goodness his smile was wide and his teeth were whiter than white. Whew! I just don't know how to describe his body. He had on a black silk tee with jeans that fit and left nothing to the imagination. He was blessed with perfect olive skin and dreads so tight someone had to be following him and twisting every day. I could see why the girls were so in love with Arc. I applaud the young lady that gets to fall in love with Carter. The young buck is nothing like his stage persona. On stage and in his music, he comes off ruff, tuff and nasty. I noticed he didn't wear a lot of jewelry, in fact he was very ordinary looking. I thought he was going to be bombarded by the girls as we walked the mall. A few did double takes but none approached him. If they only knew. Then I thought if my kids only knew. I would never ever tell them. Well I guess they may find out if they read the book. I will make sure there no free copies!

He picked a high-end restaurant called Sir Chas. They didn't bat an eye because we were both wearing jeans. Maybe someone knew who he was. The group had been in town for three days. They were scheduled to leave today, but by demand another show was added for tomorrow. We were seated immediately. He ordered "Water for the lady!" That would be me, hot damn! I needed water so bad I had to control myself. I wondered how he knew that nothing but water could quench my thirst at this moment. Now I was good to go... let the fun begin! I looked at my cell phone and noticed not one call. Arlin would never miss me and my kids were probably glad I was out of their hair.

Carter never checked his phone. I knew he had one because it was clearly visible in his well-fitting jeans.

"Is there somewhere you need to be?"

"Absolutely not!"

"Well alright then... what would you like to drink? Scratch that." He called the waiter over.

"One bottle of Dom Perion."

"I'm not a big drinker"

"No biggie I will get me a bottle to go if you don't drink it all and want a doggie bag or bottle bag." Oh, we laughed at that one.

He told me how he got into the rap game and how hard it was to make it coming from the mid-west. But he was thankful he was given the opportunity even though it meant leaving some of his old rap partners behind. I was impressed at the fact he didn't take himself too seriously and his head hadn't outgrown his body. The champagne was delicious. Carter looked at the waiter then to me and he cleared his throat.

"Would you like to eat somewhere more private?"

"Yes" Adele Bijour did not hesitate with that response and didn't care who knew it after my enthusiastic yes.

"Just where do you have in mind?" A couple of questions were answered. The restaurant was part of the hotel he was staying in and yes, they knew him and they would be providing our room service if we wanted to be alone.
"What I would like for dinner?" I wondered if I should order the little pretty girl dinner or the big fat steak I had been craving. I was being me and loving it so, I ordered the big fat, juicy well-done,

Porterhouse steak, baked potato and salad.
"You can handle that? You are a bit on the small side" then I slipped and said,

"Yea that's the chemo and now I'm ready to eat." He paused

"Alright then, let's do it." He finished giving the waiter instructions, quietly finished his drink and said in his Ricky Ricardo voice "Lucy you got some explaining to do." I was having so much fun in someone else's world.

"Do you have cancer?"

"No, I have Lupus"

"Can you explain it to me and tell me how you learned about it?"

"I'm always looking up stuff about it so over time I've stored up plenty of knowledge about the subject. I began with telling my story of having the flu for two years and what I learned thus far about it through all my research. I explained that I found it to be very interesting that there are various kinds of Lupus. However, the type I have is on the more extreme side of things. I pulled a brochure I keep in my purse and went through some of the different types of Lupus with him. I started with **Systemic Lupus** which about 70% of the people who have Lupus have the systemic form, or SLE. It's a disease in which several different body systems may be affected. With Systemic Lupus, the skin, joints, kidneys, nervous system, lungs, heart and or blood forming organs can be affected. About half of the people with Systemic Lupus have a form that affects major internal organs, particularly the kidneys. In the other half of people with Systemic Lupus, mainly the skin and joints are affected. This second type is less likely to cause serious problems."

Then we talked about **Discoid Lupus** which about 15% of people with Lupus have a form known as Discoid Lupus or Cutaneous Lupus. This form of Lupus results in a chronic rash that sometimes can cause scars. Discoid Lupus may affect the skin without affecting other organs. I was shocked that he clung to my words and actually understood what I was saying. I was hoping I hadn't scared him away with getting so technical with the information but from the look on his face he was so attentive. We continued talking.

Finally, we went through **Drug Induced Lupus** which is the least common form of Lupus develops as a result of drugs taken for other medical problems. This form is called drug induced Lupus. Signs and symptoms are similar to SLE although people with this form of Lupus rarely develop serious organ damage. Many different drugs can cause drug-induced Lupus. Signs and symptoms usually improve and disappear once the drug is stopped.

Once I understood the basics of it and what it consisted of, I began digging more into the root of it. I was trying to understand what exactly causes Lupus. It saddened me to discover that the cause of Lupus, with the exception of drug-induced Lupus, is unknown. Doctors and scientists refer to Lupus as a fish or an autoimmune disease. The immune system fights off bacteria and viruses in several ways. One way is by creating special types of blood proteins called antibodies that attack and destroy invading substances. Some researchers even believed that the various environmental factors can trigger the disease in certain people who are predisposed to it (Arthritis Foundation, 2017, Paragraph 1). I was curious why he was so interested but before I could ask, he answered.

"My favorite aunt who is like another mother to me has Lupus so I want to understand more about it. I'm wondering could they maybe have misdiagnosed her? What are some things I should look for to know if the doctors were correct?"

"Well there are only a few of the symptoms you may come across. To date no two people with Lupus would have all the same symptoms but here are the main points that you can watch out for.

- A rash across the cheeks and the bridge of the nose which they call a butterfly rash
    - Presence of specific auto antibodies measured in the blood

• Other things you may come across may be blood clots, strokes, heart attacks, eye inflammation, fever, weakness and fatigue, weight loss, Raynaud's phenomenon, muscle aches, swollen lymph nodes, loss of appetite, hair loss, Sjogren's syndrome, depression or difficulty concentrating

For more information, check out this website:
http://www.arthritispa. com/patient-info/diseases-we-treat/lupus/

But the American College of Rheumatology has developed guidelines to help doctors diagnose Lupus. If you have four or more of the listed symptoms it is likely you have Lupus or a similar condition."

"If you don't mind me asking, has it been really hard for you?"

"Yes, because it's so hard to diagnose. In the beginning, I was just relieved to have a name to what I was going through. If your mom has it she is going to need to see a rheumatologist, which is a doctor who specializes in arthritis and related diseases like Lupus. It's going to be a necessity! Once the reality of my situation set in I learned not to get frustrated when I struggled to do things that were once easy for me to do."

"Should I take her to get another opinion?"

"You can but times have changed a lot since I was diagnosed. The doctors are much more aware of Lupus. If you want my advice, my honest opinion would be if she's having any of the signs and symptoms you should get her to a second doctor as soon as possible so that they can run the proper testing and evaluations. Some people can be suffering from this disease and think they're just tired. Laboratory test will be run along with a physical exam. Unfortunately, there is no one test that can tell you whether or not you have Lupus. If they confirm Lupus as her diagnosis, as her supporter patience is also going to be very critical as you go through the process. Always keep in mind that not everyone suffers the same symptoms so you can't compare her to anyone else. She'll look normal but is going to have to pay close attention to how her body feels. You're going to have to pay close attention to her as well because she may say she's ok and not be. Look for subtle signs like the way she walks, if her skin color changes, or if she all of sudden starts moving slower than usual.

In the beginning, I had all sorts of questions and it began creating a feeling in me to want to reach out to others. I wondered where were others that had been diagnosed? Were any of them in denial? Were any of them scared? I wanted to meet people in my situation who I could talk to about how I felt and if none of them existed then I wanted to be that person for other people. I wanted to tell them to make sure they speak to their doctor and ask questions. I wanted the world to know what Lupus was so they wouldn't be afraid of speaking out about their situation. I wanted to tell them the journey is going to get extremely rough but to hang in there! Lupus is a cruel mystery, but researchers are gaining knowledge that will contribute to improvements in the quality of their life. Tell her if she ever wants to call me to talk about it she can. Us warriors have to stick together."

"Is Lupus hereditary? As a man my age am I at risk of being diagnosed with it? Will my children be at risk if I ever have any?"

"Back when I was trying to figure out where Lupus came from and was it preventable I asked my doctor some of those same questions he said he wasn't sure. I also asked if it was something that was common among my race but he wasn't sure of that either. I've read different studies trying to figure out if its hereditary. Some studies show that Lupus is not hereditary, while other studies have found that genes play an important role in the disease. The newly discovered causes of Lupus are more common in families where someone already has the disease or another related auto immune system disease, such as rheumatoid arthritis or diabetes. As I began researching my family tree I discovered that multiple people in my family had the disease as well including my mom and my daughter Adara. Most scientists believe that environmental factors, such as a virus, serves to trigger symptoms in people who have a genetic tendency to develop Lupus. So, to answer your question as a man your age yes you and your children are at risk if your aunt is diagnosed because you will have the traits within your family.

For the questions that are unanswered I research every day because as new changes come about I'm hoping to discover something that can help Adara. As of now most of my knowledge has come from reading things published by the Arthritis Foundation of America and the Lupus Foundation of America. Tell your aunt they both are great resources that can help her if she ever needs it. Here's their information if either of you ever want to call them with any questions or concerns. The Lupus foundation of America at 1-800-558-0121 and the Arthritis foundation of America at 1-800-283-7800." I hoped I was able to help him help his aunt.

As we talked we started walking. We took the long way around to the hotel. He reached for my hand and surely, I thought I would die! One of the final clues that my marriage to Arlin was over was when we were on one of our Saturday night dates and we were walking through a mall headed for the movie theater. I reached out to hold his hand and he almost violently snatched away. It felt so good to be walking hand in hand with this young man. By now I had stopped referring to him as a boy. As we walked through the elegant, finely decorated in a modern motif of Christ of Evon hotel, we ran into his manager.

Carter introduced me as Adele Bijour. No one had ever said my name like that. Even I felt important. His manager Rick was sweet and nice looking. He had an accent but I couldn't put my finger on it either. We talked for a moment then headed to his room for dinner. I was sure he was stalling so that dinner would be there when we got there. Did I say room? There is no button for his floor in the elevator. Yes sir, it was the penthouse! I tried to be cool but the look on my face said it all.

"Is the whole entourage staying in here?" He laughed

"No, they are in a block of rooms below."

Then I saw the dining room table, completely dressed for us and the two Adele kickers... two dozen red roses and chocolate covered strawberries! Where did he come from? Had Carter been in my dreams all these years? I wanted to yell "I am in love", but I knew better and knew it wasn't true or possible. But, damn was I in love with this feeling! We sat at the table starring at each other saying nothing. He leaned over and kissed me on the cheek... I am sure to see my reaction. I cupped his beautiful face in both hands and kissed him so soft, so hard and so long his reaction couldn't be hidden. There was too much stuff on the table so the floor did just fine.

We finally made it to the swanky bedroom. I felt like I was in a movie. I wondered if this was a set up and I was being recorded or something, but then I said the hell with it. I am playing all nine innings of this game. I didn't think this young man could know so much about pleasing a woman. He knew what to say, what to do, what to touch, what to kiss... He definitely knew what he was doing. After hours of lovemaking he asked,

"Adele, you still wanting that steak?"

"No thanks I've had my share."

"I'll call and get dinner ordered again"

"No, I'm totally satisfied." I said as I laid in this ceiling high four poster bed enjoying the luxury of its covering. I am having a quiet conversation with myself. Ms. Adele was thinking maybe this was the kind of manic episodes she needed more often. I was fully aware my behavior was that of a manic episode. I could have controlled it but I didn't want to. I was so hungry for love and attention there no way I was going to shut that down.

Carter was up walking around and I heard him on the phone. Then he was in the bathroom and I could hear water running. He came back to bed and started asking me a number of questions. He was concerned as whether or not he had hurt me in any way. I told him if I was going to die tonight this is how I wanted to go. We talked some more about Lupus. I pretty much told him all I knew, which was a lot. I felt so empowered being able to educate someone and bring awareness to this wolf disease that resides within many of us. My prayer was that by sharing what I knew I was able to repay him a little bit for all the joy he had given me on this day. He wanted me to connect with his aunt Bev. How amazing!

He went into the bathroom again and came out with the hotel robe. I laughed because I am obsessed with those long oversized white robes. He put me in it and led me to the bath. Oh, my! I had never seen anything like it! There were rose petals leading to the bath for two and an ornate table with champagne and chocolate covered strawberries. I never wanted this day to end. We soaked and talked for hours it seemed. After turning into prunes, he slowly dried me off as I did him. He kissed my hand and led me back to the dining room of the penthouse where there was a full meal laid out, but this time breakfast. It was just amazing how someone could be so caring and thoughtful. We sat and ate but mostly smiled, joked and laughed. I had told him my full story so he knew I had a husband and family I was running away from.

"Do you have to be leaving soon?"

"Do you want me to stay longer?"

"Yes"

"I'll just check in with one of the kids in case someone was looking for me. It's not likely anyone is looking for me. My phone hasn't rung once and I've been gone since eight yesterday morning."

That made him a bit sad, but not so sad that he couldn't pick me up and carry me to the freshly made bed. I swear this cougar's little man didn't miss a beat. Carter was more of a man than any old fart I had ever encountered. We made love like it was the last time, over and over again. Sadly it would be the last time. It was getting to be pretty late in the morning. The time had come for me to leave. I had no idea what part of the mall I was in or where my van was parked. I remembered I pulled my parking ticket when I was first talking to him, but I don't know what happened to it. I got up to freshen up a little, but not too much. I wanted his smell to stay with me as long as possible.

"How on earth am I going to ever find my van?"

"No worries I got you. When you're ready its waiting for you at the front door." I didn't question him. He made everything else happen... why not this?

Truthfully, I felt very old driving a full-size van. At least it didn't look like a minivan. It was time to say goodbye because he had a sound check to get to. Meanwhile, I had an empty house to get to. He laughed as he invited me to his show that night. I was like yeah right and laughed. He said, "well if you want your kids to come, I will leave four tickets at will call." This experience was something I would cherish every day for the rest of my life. I left Carter with a soft kiss on his cheek.

Sure, enough when I got downstairs there sat my big black and tan van with one of his crew behind the wheel. He got out and said "Thank you. You will never know what you did for my guy. Enjoy the goodies... later!" I had no idea what he was talking about. Maybe the future would hold the key. I looked behind me and there were all sorts of bags, red roses and boxes. I had to be cool and drive off before I checked it out. I decided I would just go on home and check it out there. I was sure no one would be there.

Yippee... I was home. The drive wasn't long enough. No cars were on the streets and I was sure Arlin wasn't home. He probably got home just in time to go to work and was glad I wasn't there. When the fun began I saw the roses, three pair of red bottom heels, jeans, tops, dresses, tennis shoes and jewelry! Man... I went shopping and didn't have to shop! Of course, there was a giant box of chocolate covered strawberries. He must have found my sizes in my clothes and shoes, since he picked them up from the floor and hung them up. There was a note that said

Carter,

I hated hearing your story and that you felt you were less than. Your family will someday know your worth and they will be sorry. You are the strongest lady I have ever had the pleasure of meeting. Lady, you turned a brother out! You were a ray of sunshine in my life. I am forever grateful to have met you. I can only pray that the universe will see fit to bring us together again. I will be watching out for you my dearest Adele Bijour.

> *Forever my heart,*
> *Carter*
> *Talk to you soon*

Chapter 10

THE ENDING

It was a good day for a change. The house was in order, dinner was in the oven, I was feeling good and Arlin was home. I was totally caught off guard in thinking Arlin and I could have a nice conversation. However, I noticed whichever direction I went, he went the other way. He was pacing and nice yet a bit nervous.

"Is everything alright?"

"Yes" he whispered." It was like we were following one another around the house.

If I was in the kitchen then he went upstairs or were circling the stairwell. In my mind, something was wrong and he wasn't ready to talk. I was remembering that eerie feeling when one of his friends was killed in the line of duty. At that time we both just walked in circles until we both just sat on the floor and cried. I just could not imagine what was going on with him.

As I made my pass to the living room, Arlin spoke.

"Adele, I need to talk to you. Would you sit down?" He didn't sit. He just stood on the other side of our huge dining room. Silence, silence and more silence. I am a talker so it was killing me to be quiet. The boom finally fell when Arlin looked at me.

"Baby I can't keep doing this to you...I want a divorce and I'm moving out." I was stunned even though this should have been good news. I had conditioned myself that this was the life I was sentenced to, so to change my routine was scary. I did not cry.

"Why now?"

"I was wrong for treating the way I did and you deserved better."

I couldn't think of what would have been better? He owned up to all the years of infidelities and women getting in my face. He told me how sorry he was for what he did to me. Out of nowhere I found myself apologizing for everything I had done to him. I wasn't guilt free in this awful relationship. I had my share of faults, affairs to get back at him and spending money like there was no tomorrow. I just figured it all balanced out. He just kept saying how sorry he was. Finally I yelled at him, "yeah it takes a sorry ass mother fucker to do some shit like this!" It was a good thing that big ass table separated us because I am positive I would have slapped the living shit out of him. Now after all these years of playing this game, he was sorry.

I left the table without another word. I went to bed to try and figure out why this was happening. Before going upstairs to bed, I told him dinner would be ready shortly and to please take it out of the oven and make sure the kids ate when they got home. He said, "okay babe..." *Did he say, "okay babe"?* Was I dreaming? What the hell? Then the kids came in and they were full of joy because they got dad instead of their mom. I could hear him and the kids talking and laughing. Abella and Bryce were so happy to have him all to themselves... my poor babies.

I began to wonder how I was going to take care of them, how was I going to take care of myself, what about insurance, my house, my mother... We can't live on what I get from social security. All I could think of was how I failed at a failed marriage... how embarrassing. So much went through my mind. Could I do this? How would I face his family? I suspected his mom would be full of happiness for her son. Whatever he wanted... she wanted. After all this time, I couldn't believe this is what things had come to. The things I did for his family, the money I spent on his family... if Arlin only knew.

My mind continued to race until he entered the bedroom

disrupting my train of thought. I didn't know what was going to happen. Was he leaving now? Had he changed his mind? Then he spoke

"The kids are good, food is put away, I left you a plate in the microwave and the dishwasher is loaded and running. I'm going to take the kids out for ice cream. They'll be back soon."

"We're going to have to have a sit-down meeting to work this all out... the when, where and how."

"Babe whatever you want to do, just let me know."

This is some weird shit! I thought to myself. He didn't take any clothes or anything. He was trusting I wasn't one of those crazy ass women that would tear up all of his shit. But, that's not my M.O. and he knew that. I cared about my dignity! As a matter of fact, I cared about my dignity so much that I took enough pills to kill an elephant as soon as I heard the door close. I was out cold within minutes. The last thing I heard was the garage door opening and closing.

Hours later I woke up to the dog barking and Arlin sleeping next to me with his arms around me. I was groggy and not sure of where I was or if I was dead or just dreaming. I was awake enough to know I was pissed at myself. So, I took another handful of pills and I made sure to empty the bottles and wash them down with the water. I always kept them on my nightstand and I was out again. The next time I woke up I was in the hospital. DAMN!!! In all these years of my craziness I always avoided being hospitalized for it. I was in the emergency room with Dr. Anderson standing over me.

"Girl, am I going to have to lock your butt up in the nut ward?"

"No, please don't! It was just a mistake, nothing I was trying to do, I just wanted to sleep after Arlin told me he wanted a divorce." I pleaded with him.

"That idiot wants a divorce? What about you and the two younger kids?"

"I just needed to rest and clear my mind to figure out what I am going to do."

"Okay, you can go home but I need you see Carlita today. She will call you with a time. You have to take care of yourself and no asshole of a man is worth nothing more than a kick in the ass."

I was laughing through my anger. Although I was mad as hell that I failed to leave my miserable life, I laughed that I had doc's sympathy and that he bought my story. While waiting for my discharge papers, I sat trying to figure out how I got here. Out of nowhere, in walks Bennett just as straight faced as usual.

"Are you ready to go or are you going to be admitted?"

"Going home"

Looking impatient, Bennett just stared at me. It was a silent ride home and he just dropped me off at the front door and said,

"See you later... do you need anything?"

"No and if I did, I wouldn't ask you."

He was definitely Arlin's son. His way with the women was cool and smooth. On more than one occasion Arlin had tried to move in on Bennett's lady friends. I hope Bennett finds happiness in his life.

Not long after I got home, Adara came in with Abella and Bryce. They were very happy they didn't have to stay with their grandmother. Whenever I was in the hospital, Arlin's mom always demanded they come by her. Bryce didn't mind one way or another, but Abella just hated being left there. She never gave a reason until she was older, but I always felt her pain. She was shy and wouldn't speak up for herself. Adara fed the kids then they all came to rest in my bed with me. Arlin was working.

Arlin left me in bed dying. To this day, I don't know if he knew I had taken all those pills and whether or not he really just left me there to die. His story was that when he woke up he just figured I was in a deep sleep. He got the kids off to school and went on to work. However, he never came to the hospital when Adara called him and I am sure he was disappointed to see me when he got home. I guess it was an act of the universe that Adara came by and wondered why I was sleeping so hard without much movement. Normally when I took a nap during the day I turned the alarm on. My dog Polar was outside, ringing the back doorbell trying to get in. Yes, my pooch Polar knew how to ring the doorbell when he wanted to come in. Chow chows have a lot of fur and can't stand being outside when it's too hot out, but he would stay out all day if it was cold. Adara finally figured something was wrong. She knew I was in trouble after she shook the life back into me and poured my pitcher of water in my face. I finally started coming around. I looked at her and said, "the gorillas are painting the garage and they need help!" With that statement she dialed 911.

The next few days were quiet. I was having a hard time keeping my thoughts straight. My body was truly tired and I had no idea if I could get through this. I had been seeing my therapist Carlita quite often, even talking to her late nights on the phone. I had to be really careful with what I said her, which meant I could not be totally honest. However, if I was honest I would have told her that at my first opportunity I planned to kill myself. I remember telling her I wish I could just fall out on her office floor and cry. Her response was "what's stopping you?" So, I did... I cried for thirty minutes and when the tears dried up I looked up at her and said, "I can't do this, why is this so hard?" She set up in her rocking chair, looked at me over her glasses and said, "what makes you so special that you shouldn't have to go through hard times? Everyone has to go through something." With that I got up and sat back in my seat. I am sure if I would have been completely honest with her the response would have been different and she would have had me confined because I was a danger to myself. So, I had to always go through my suicidal thoughts alone. I was just not going to be locked up on the psychiatric ward.

So, I always made my life harder. I did however agree to outpatient group sessions. They always ended with the facilitator contacting Carlita because they were concerned. I quickly learned what I could and could not say. At the time, I was diagnosed as a level one manic bipolar. I had pretty good control though. I lived everyday controlling my urges and that was not easy. I had an image to live up to. I think I would take the physical part of Lupus over the mental. The boatloads of medications I was on were known to cause depression and some increased suicidal tendencies and of course Lupus caused its own depression. If the people around me only knew the hell I was living.

I thought it was time to face the music... so, I put my professional face on, drew up some notes about our divorce and even set a move out date. As we sat at the dining room table across from one another, I gave Arlin an opportunity to change his mind. The first thing out of my mouth was

"Are you sure?"

"Yes" he responded embarrassingly. All that was on my mind was being sick, losing his insurance and of course the paycheck. I started pleading with him.

"Please let's try this one more time. I won't say anything about what you do. I'll just be quiet. You can even take over the bills and check book. You can just move into the lower level. Just please don't bring any of your women into our house." There was silence. I had to get control of myself and the tears because I didn't deserve to be treated this way.

Once I gathered myself I started again. We set the date and split up our things. I said, "I would rather not tell the kids until the move out day." He agreed. One thing we did not discuss was money. At least I don't remember it. I do remember him coming by each week and putting a check in the mail slot. One of the most difficult days for me was when he was moving. I was heartbroken as I sat at the dining room table watching twenty years go out the door. He had his nephews helping him and they couldn't look me in the eyes at all. Arlin was so far gone in his head wanting to be free that he kicked the two older kids Adara and Bennett out of the apartment above his mom just so he would have some place to go.

Although that was low down, I'm sure he was thinking they could just move back home. But either way, karma is a bitch and he would eventually get his. Even if it took a couple years.

During the early divorce times, I came home and ran right into Arlin. "Why are you here?" I asked. Apparently, he was there on a regular basis. So, the next day I had the locks changed which brought out the monster in him and lead to an explosive telephone conversation. He made it clear he was taking the house, the kids and could care less what happened to me. I was a nervous wreck. I needed a lawyer and fast! I was volunteering at the courthouse and the person I was working for gave me the name of a good one. She also told me about her affair with Arlin!

I felt like I always had to look over my shoulder because I never knew what to expect. One day I happened to be driving Arlin's truck and a woman tried to run into me head on! I pulled over and got out. I could hear her calling him all kinds of names until she saw me with the baton. She ran back to her car and took off.

As I am sharing my stories I think it is truly a miracle I am still here. I chose to share, not for sympathy but for strength. I pray that through my tales, one must always know that you can overcome anything. It is a matter of how you choose to direct and personally plan your life. Lupus is driven by stress and honestly that could be why I suffered so badly with it. My life was a book of stress that I would not wish upon anyone. Personal planning is key.

When I met the lawyer the first thing he said was cops always win, but he would do his best. The process went rather quickly and yes, Arlin won. The most hilarious part of the proceedings was Arlin challenging me on whether or not I had Lupus. His attorney said Arlin had Lupus because he had a rash on his leg, which could have been true. Rashes on the skin are called discoid Lupus, but not as serious as SLE. While researching, I found the letter to Dr. Anderson trying to get him to say I didn't have Lupus and I was totally capable of working. That hurt, but Dr. Anderson did not fail me and he told a story that I can't repeat. The judge asked me what I wanted and my response was "my house". He asked how I was going to keep it up. I was so scared and nervous, but that's the only thing I could think of. I was still trying to keep my dignity. Child support, alimony and social security disability... in my mind I could make it work. Now the master of my life, Lupus was back and in high gear. I went to bed for weeks except to get my babies off to school. Money for food was short and I had no energy to cook.

I remember Mickey D's had a two-dollar deal with two burgers, fries and a drink. So, I would order that for the kids and just add two sodas. One night after the kid's nutritious meal, I went to my bedroom and sat in the window seat because I could no longer bear the pain in my heart. I decided to page Carlita. I needed help. When she returned my call, my mind flipped the script. I told her I was having a tough time because Abella wouldn't stop crying and that made me even sadder. She knew me well. She said, "get off the shit, what's going on?" Do you need to go in? I thought about it, but I didn't want to give Arlin any more ammunition for court. Lord please help me was my thought. I so wanted to tell my therapist how badly I wanted to kill myself and take my two youngest babies with me. I just needed to talk, but I was so afraid. Never in a billion years would I ever say that to her. My babies would be taken from me and I would be confined.

I couldn't bear the thought of leaving my babies in this world without me even though I knew they would be taken care of. If nothing else Arlin Hamilton was a good dad. I had a plan in place that would cause no pain or mess, just peace, I hoped. I thought the time was near. After a useless talk with Carlita, I couldn't go on. I could not look into their eyes and see a mother that failed them looking back. Abella was having a more difficult time than Bryce. She was so angry with her dad she barely spoke anymore. She didn't want anything to do with him and of course I got blamed. As a matter of fact, I got blamed for everything. Arlin told anyone who would listen that I put him out on the street and took everything from him. As I sat in the window seat, I kept searching my mind wondering how my life could be so awful. What had I done in my life that was so bad that I was living in a form of hell? I could only come up with things that were done to me.

I thought back to the two times I was raped. I wondered if I did something wrong? The answer had to be no. I was only guilty of having brothers that had friends. Those two occurrences didn't seem to cause as much pain as this divorce was causing. I was left blaming God. I knew it was what they called a storm and I knew God would put you through storms. But, I was feeling like "Damn!

Is He going come get me? Please save me... someone!" I made it through the night because my pills for sleep took away the anxiety and I was okay.

I was given a little shelter from my storm. I guess I was given a boost. In my next meeting with Carlita she jumped right in. "You better not be thinking of involving those kids!" I told her I was ok and that I was still a work in progress... not healed in day but healed enough to wait for the next day. I cut our time short. It was too much thinking. Arlin approached me smugly when he picked up the kids and told me I should get rid of the van because it's going to need work. He said I shouldn't call him because he wouldn't help out if I had van trouble. I didn't respond.

On my next good day, I took his advice and went and got myself a new car. The divorce wasn't final so I used his information to get my car. My first new car... I loved that prize! I dressed it up and started driving again. It was a stick shift and it made me feel like I had a little control. It only had five miles on it! My time in the bed became less as I was trying to force myself to feel better. I had to stop feeling sorry for myself and start living the best life I could.

I decided that it was a great time to put my new car, "Arc" on the road to Mississippi to see my mom. That trip gave me new life and a somewhat angry attitude. I think I can thank Tupac for giving me the strength and courage to say "FUCK'EM ALL!" I and that double disc became inseparable, always ending with "BETTER DAYZ." I was coming back. The divorce started making me feel like I needed a man in my life on occasion. I think in some kind of lame way of keeping up with Arlin I played around for a while, but that just left me feeling empty.

I wasn't answering the phone anymore so people started showing up at my door. One person in particular, my cousin, was determined to drag me out of the bed and take me to church. She promised that her Pastor would watch over me... no strings no pressure.

So, I began my search for God again.

Chapter 11

THE BIG MOVE

I tried, but I just couldn't swing keeping the house. My biggest foe was my manic episodes. I would still spend money like it was nothing and then go to bed depressed. The Lupus had taken a turn for the good and that made me mad because I couldn't shop! I came up with a few ways to keep money coming in. I thought about renting out a room, but that was a big no because I needed my privacy. Then I went back to the bank part time in the call center. That lasted a few months and then the Lupus returned. I found that whatever I tried, I was only good for a few weeks and then my body would shut down.

I started speaking at small health functions and that would bring in a few dollars, but I would spend that before I got home. Then came the idea of becoming a foster parent. I went to the classes and researched the process, but when I found out the amount that would be provided... I was out! Not worth my time. I decided taking care of me, Abella and Bryce was all I could handle.

Then the bright idea of selling weed popped up! I had never been into drugs or alcohol, but during this lonely time I had reconnected with one of my favorite cousins. Ulysses was there for me. He suggested I smoke a joint. He figured that might help my pain and relax me so I took him up on that offer. I took the first joint he gave me, went to the garage, took a couple of hits and lost my mind! I had to crawl back into to house. The next time I saw him I had questions.

"What on earth did you give me?"

"Awe cuz I don't play, I only have the best."

"Well Ulysses your best is too good for me, and it made me sick."

I began thinking Bennett and Adara had more than enough friends that I could supply. So, I looked up another relative. My nephew was a known drug dealer. We started hanging out and I gave him the run down on me and Arlin. To my surprise, after he heard the story he had much to say.

"You know I can have him taken out." I admit I thought about it really hard. Then I realized my child support and alimony would be gone.

"No, he is not worth it." So, my dude gave me a gun and taser.

"Always keep both of these with you." Then it was on to business.

"I would rather sell it for you and give you your profit so you don't get into any trouble."

"Yes and no... meaning I'll pay for the whole amount and keep some for myself and see if I could build up base."

Deal closed! It was a good thing we did it that way because I gave it all away. That manic in me wouldn't allow me to hold on to anything. I wanted everyone to be happy. I did give away a good chunk to one of Bennett's friend. Arlin had moved his stripper girlfriend in with him and that pissed me off. So, I asked Looney for a favor. Arlin's girl had a junkie car she always parked in front of the house. Good old Looney came up with the idea he would steal the car and take it around the corner and take the doors off and flatten the tires. That was hilarious! After My Dude gave me my share, my drug dealing days were over.

It was Christmas time and the house went on the market. The timing was nice because the house was decorated and every time there was a showing, I baked cookies and set them on the island. It didn't take long before an offer was in and accepted. Moving in January in Minneapolis was a nightmare. It was a big house and there was a lot to get rid of. Now the hunt was on to find an apartment for me and the two kids. I was shocked that we kept getting turned down or we needed a cosigner. It was so frustrating because I was trying to find a pet friendly place. It came down to two places outside of the city limits but close to the kid's school. The one place we really had our hearts set on allowed dogs and they would take a chow. Well of course the heartaches kept coming. We were again turned down and now I was scared. The community next door accepted us with a cosigner. My cousin that had been helping me get my act together cosigned and gave me the upfront money due.

Moving day had arrived and I wasn't ready. Everyone was yelling, the dog was barking and my sister was trying to run things, which made it worse. I couldn't get Bryce or Abella to pack their rooms. It was as if they refused to go. I still had not made a decision about Polar. During the showings, a lady was very interested in him and she gave me her number in case I decided to get rid of him. That was tough because Chows are normally one owner dogs. Polar was so cute. He was mean but he was my baby. He had a bad habit of peeing on men, especially cops in uniform.

I finally reached my breaking point and I didn't care who saw me melt because I could not do another thing. I was done and I did not care how anything got done. All I could think about was my fluffy white Polar. I think they had to roll me out of my bed and to this day I don't know how they got Bryce and Abella packed. They kept bugging me about the dog so, finally I made the call and she agreed to come pick him up. It broke my heart. We finally got out after two days of moving. Stuff was going all over town.

It came time to close on the house. Arlin had to be there to sign off so, they had him come in early to sign his portion. What I soon found out was I was in the hole! I had to pay to sell my house and I felt lower than low. There were past due taxes, water bills and all kind of other stuff that there were liens for. I couldn't believe it! My realtor had to lend me money to close. My heart just ached and when I finally got back in the car I cried like there was no tomorrow. That was why I could not get anyone to rent to us.

We were in our new place doing nothing, but staring at boxes. I always knew to get the bedrooms set up first, so that was our chore. Beds only...I didn't care about anything else. Then I got the dreaded phone call I knew was coming. Polar wasn't working out. I had to go get him right away. I drove to his new home without a plan. The kids had asked their dad if he would take him. I knew he would say no because that was my dog. Polar stayed by my side and slept in bed with me until Arlin came home. Then he would literally kick him out of the bed as hard as he could. I hated Arlin for that. I knew I was going to have to take him to the Humane Society. I got there and he was standing in the doorway looking. I called out "Polar" and oh my goodness... he came running so hard and fast he knocked me down in the snow. Joy, joy, joy! He cried as he kissed me. We laid in the snow for maybe twenty minutes. I saw this woman looking out the window, so I finally got up and went to the door.

She said he had never shown any emotion while he was there. He wouldn't obey and he was just mean. I said "I know... don't apologize. They are one owner dogs." I gathered up my baby and he couldn't wait to get into the car. As we rode around the city he was so happy. All I could think of was where I was taking him. I didn't know if I could do it. When I went in I filled out all the paper work and tried to make him seem nice in hopes that he could be adopted. At the end of the form it asked if I wanted to be notified if he's adopted or put down. Stupid me, I wanted to know. The next day that phone call came. Polar had snapped on a number of staff and would not let anyone come near him, so he was put down. Throughout this whole divorce process, I had never shed as many tears as I did on this day.

Sharing this part of my life has been very difficult, but my point would be helping someone take something from my journey and do it different in yours. Systemic Lupus Erythematosus will ride with you every step you take in your life. It will make easy things more difficult and hard things will seem like the end of the world. Everything you do, say or think will have some reflection of how you deal with Lupus.

Chapter 12

THE ROAD TO MISSISSIPPI

I remember that time in my life so very clearly. My mom wanted me to come and visit her in Mississippi. I said I would even though I was feeling very sick. She made the stipulation that I come alone and that meant definitely not to bring my sister. One time I made the mistake of bringing my sister with me for a visit. My mother was so mad she could hardly speak the entire time we were there. They had an awful relationship. It's what drove my mom back to Mississippi after my father died. I told mom I was in bad shape and to give me a couple of days to get there. It took me three tries before I could get in the car to head for Mississippi. I knew that something was going on for her to make that kind of request of me knowing how sick I was. She would never ask of me anything that she didn't think I was capable of. She was always very concerned about my health and my well-being. Not feeling well was an understatement.

On my first try, I raised my head to get going on this trip, but my body just wouldn't let me. My head ached like a bull dozier was coming through. My back hurt because of the kidney disease I was recently diagnosed with caused by the Lupus. I was running a temperature of 102.1 and every bone in my body hurt. When I called mom and she asked if I was on my way. I felt so bad that I had to tell her I was still in bed. I could hear the disappointment in her voice. I had hoped that she would let me off the hook, but no such luck. "Well when you get up and get on your way call me", said Mama Adara in that firm voice. Now I knew this trip was important. The next time I woke up it was 10 p.m. that night and she was calling again.

I sucked it up and told her to please give another day and I'd leave out at 3 a.m. She said, "ok just don't bring anyone with you, so wait till you feel better." She sounded as if she was giving up on me and that hurt. I tried to get up right then and head out. I got my bag packed, music together, showered and dressed. My body was still telling me no. I laid down for a few minutes and that few minutes turned into hours. I did not call her. On my third try I just went numb to my body and ignored what I was feeling. I finally called her after leaving the state of Minnesota and entering Wisconsin. There was joy in her voice and cries of agony coming from my body, but I was happy and relieved. I never once thought I couldn't make it to my mother.

My mom was so special that we named our first daughter after her and our second daughter after her as well. As Adara and Abella grew to know their grandma Adara, they took great pride in knowing they were named after their granny. She taught them their first song... Take me out to the ballgame. She was a huge Chicago Cubs fan and loved the seventh inning stretch with Harry Carey singing her song. She was a character. A Jehovah's Witness that could tell you off better than a drunken sailor and she loved music I don't know if there was a particular type of music that she did not love. She made lots of friends in the music industry and at one point she even owned a record shop. I was so proud of that record shop. It had put Victoria on the map with some of the industry's biggest stars. Since she was friends with all the DJs from the radio stations we always got our pick of tickets to concerts when the big stars would come to Minneapolis. Because of my mom I met a lot of stars and one of my biggest joys was getting to go backs stage when Earth, Wind and Fire came to town. I got to see the Jackson Five too! When I didn't go back stage we always had front row seats and I was so proud to be at a concert with my mom.

While running this record shop my mom became kind of a neighborhood therapist who gave advice to many and helped many. There was a time that the record shop had to move across town to help the city. It was located across from the train station and my mom decided that she would serve coffee and rolls to the people waiting on the train to go to work in the city. There are just not enough words I can say about my mommy. Now, don't get me wrong. She could be mean as heck. You did not mess with Miss

Adara. She took no mess from anyone, but she was a great woman.

Mama Adara was always kind of sickly, but that never stopped her from doing what she had to do. By trade she was a registered dietitian at the local hospital. She retired from that hoping to relax, but from there she went on to take care of a number of people in the family. She always caught herself holding her breath for the next new business venture my father would bring home. First, he had the bright idea of the record shop that she ended up running. Then he decided he would turn it into a grocery store to help the neighborhood and she ended up running that as well. They ran more than one restaurant, more than one coffeehouse and carried a number of different business ventures.

My father was the kind of guy who would be in love with an idea and tell her he would run the business venture. But after a couple weeks, he would get bored and she would have to take it over. She was smart and just that kind of person... she was amazing. My dad always said he was going to make a million dollars and he did, but he spent it. My father, rest his grumpy soul, was not the nicest man. He was quite mean to my mom and I hated him for that. When he died I did not shed a tear. All I could remember was the abuse he put upon my mom.

Oh, excuse me... I have totally gone off track of what I wanted to share with you. I wanted to share with you the trip to Mississippi, but when I start talking about my mama Adara nothing else matters.

Chapter 13

ARRIVING BACK HOME

Phone calls to summon me to come to Mississippi, finally successful, I made the arrangements for the kids to stay with Arlin, packed my music and a small suitcase. I hit the road for Mississippi. I was looking forward to a very peaceful ride as I thought about what she could possibly want. I had time to think about where my life was now that I was divorced and I thought about how sick I was on the journey. The road was long and I had no one to talk to. Just my imagination and memories. The first memory to pop up was my marriage to Arlin. My mom loved that man so much that I still don't know who took the divorce harder, me or her. She loved and trusted him more than her own four sons. She could always count on him. One day she calmly told me that as soon as Arlin could get the women and the streets out of his system, he would be back and that I should be patient.

Then I remembered one of our many conversations. We spoke on the phone every day, sometimes two or three times a day. It was one of those conversations she slipped up in. She said "oh I saw my oncologist today..." When she realized she had slipped she tried to keep going, but I stopped her. I said "Whoa! Wait a minute lady... your oncologist? What do you mean oncologist? What's going on? Tell me now!" Her response was reserved as she said "I have lymphoma." That was all she said. "Mom aren't you going to tell me what this is... what it's about or anything?" She said "No, not really. It's just something to do with my glands." I knew better than to press her at that moment and she knew well that I was going to research and get my answers. I was going to figure out what it was on my own so, we left that discussion right there.

As I was driving along on my road trip, I wondered if this was the reason she was calling for me to come to her. A part of me was a bit pissed because I was feeling so bad and no one was acknowledging my pain. But, in that moment reality kicked in. This trip was not about me. I needed to focus on my journey and put Lupus on hold, at least in my mind. I willed my body to gain strength and to freeze so I could concentrate on just using the tools I needed to make this drive. The headache never left but the music put me at ease. Everything else just became invisible. The only time this became a problem was when I had to stop for the restroom. Because my kidneys were inflamed that chore was beyond painful and so was getting in and out of the car and walking. I was miserable. Another thought popped up! When I was on the speaking circuit for Lupus, I always described Lupus as a disease that doesn't usually kill you. It just made your life miserable. This trip held true to my words.

Then suddenly out of nowhere the rain began falling... falling like there was no tomorrow. I could not even see the front end the car. I was so scared. The rain was so heavy I could not see how to pull off to the side of the road. It seemed as if all the cars had just stopped in place and no one knew what to do. At that point, all I could do was pray to God, thank Him and ask for forgiveness for my life. Now, I found myself telling Arlin how much I loved him and that I was sorry for everything we had gone through. I was screaming for my kids telling each and every one of them how much I loved them. I told Adara I loved her and that it would be ok, told Bennett to be strong and that he was ok, I screamed to Abella I love you baby, I love you and cried out to Bryce you are my baby you are my baby Bryce! And as I was going through a rainstorm I had never experienced before, I cried out to my mom to let her know I was trying to get there. "I am trying to get there... wait for me mommy! I want to be there! I don't want to let you down mommy!"

I was in a full-blown panic attack and I needed help immediately! I said "Lord Jesus help me! Help me to see my way". Then I found myself saying that prayer that everybody says when they think their life is over. "God if you get me out of this I will never do anything wrong again. Please Lord please get me out of this!" And at that moment I'm drove under a bridge so there was a pause in the rain and I breathed a sigh of relief wishing the bridge would never end. Of course it did, but on the other side was sunshine and not a drop of rain! Not one drop of rain! I'm sure the other drivers were as stunned as I was. As I gathered my bearings I realized that Tupac was playing on my CD player. I'm not a big rap fan but this double disc was so insightful. The song that was playing was "Better Days". When I say that CD was very insightful I realized that track kept replaying all while I was going through that storm. After I had driven a couple of miles the song changed and I hadn't touched anything. As a matter of fact, when I changed my music I changed it to gospel. All I could say was thank you Lord.

My entire thought process had changed for the rest of my trip. My thoughts were about hope and being positive no matter the storm. I thought about what I could do when I got home. What I would say to the kids and how I would change my interaction with them. I thought about what I was going to say to my mom and what I was going to do with my mom.

I love the little city that she lived in. My dream was to move to a small friendly city in the south. I knew there were a lot of things going on in the city because this is the Fourth of July holiday time. I was glad to get away from home because I had no one to share the holidays with anymore. The kids are always with Arlin on holidays. I was usually left alone at home. Maybe this Fourth of July might be a little bit more exciting. We would soon find out.

The 18 hour drive starting to come to an end. My body was still on auto pilot. I couldn't believe I made this trip all alone. My stops were calculated because I had to drive straight through. Since my mommy has not told me what she wanted with me, I couldn't afford to waste another moment. I knew I had to get there. The sun was starting to go down and I knew I had to make it through the darkest area of Jackson. There are no lights on the two-lane highway... just t total blackness. If you got caught going through there at night it was like something from a movie. This was always my scariest time going to Mississippi to get caught in that darkness. It wasn't dark yet but it was time to put the pedal to the metal and hope for no troopers. My mom called and asked me how far was I and I told her I was close. I'd be there in an hour and I could hear the joy in her voice.

During this road trip, I thought about Lupus and how my life had been affected by it, but how my body was reacting was not a concern. Even though at one of my bathroom stops I could see the rashes that had taken over my body. My face was red as tomatoes, my hands hurt, I could barely walk and I don't think I had thought to eat during the entire trip. I was leaning against a wall trying to regain my strength to get back to the car and a lady asked if I was okay. I said "yes, I've just got to get to my mom." She said "sweetie you don't look very good. I hope you are not alone." I responded "no I am not alone. I'll be okay." As I was headed for the door this lady came running to me with the biggest Pepsi I'd ever seen! I didn't have time to stop for a drink. Even funnier was Pepsi was my mom's drink of choice. I thanked her and she walked with me to the car. She said "I knew you were alone." I replied "no I'm not... my God would never leave me alone." She smiled. As I gently got in the car, I looked up through the open sunroof and said thank you God for being my passenger. I looked at this giant Pepsi said thank you Lord.

I finally reached Highway 20. Familiar sights were making themselves known and I was excited. As I rounded the curve I could see the sun going down quickly and I thanked God I made it through Jackson without the darkness. Around the curves I could see the mall, all my little favorite stores even my favorite shaved ice shack. I was here. I had made it! I turned the corner on Market Street and past the gas station and my favorite parking space was available. I saw my mom's building and I backed my little car into my space right next to my mom's car. I sat there with tears running down my face because I had made it. I accomplished a goal. I didn't let my mom down. When I looked straight ahead the sun was setting just as I pulled into the parking space. The most beautiful sight I will ever see in my life again... my Mississippi sunset.

I got out of the car very slowly, not sure whether or not my legs would carry me to the door. I knew I was in a full-blown Lupus flare, but this trip wasn't about me. By the end of this trip it will be drilled into my head that it wasn't about me. I finally made it to the door and opened it to my beautiful mama and her beautiful flowing head of grey hair running down her back. She was sitting in her chair and ever so nonchalantly she said "what took you so long?" We laughed and laughed and laughed. She asked "did you bring any bags with you?"

"Yep it's in the car, but I didn't have enough strength to bring it in." She said "that doesn't matter... you've got everything you need here anyway." I responded "that's why I only bring a small bag." Then this woman who had been calling me every few miles to see how far away I was says, "well now you're here... I'm going to bed. Good night, I love you and I'm glad you came alone." That's my mom. I guessed I would have to see what tomorrow would bring. She made my bed with my favorite comforter set and freshly scented sheets. For me, a shower was coming up and sleep to follow.

Chapter 14

QUALITY TIME WITH MOM

After hours and hours of sleep I finally arose to the smell of my mommy making grits. Grits are not a hard thing to make but they're very easy to mess up and no one can make grits like my mommy! She didn't bother making all the other things that go along with breakfast because she knew that all I needed was my bowl of grits and a piece of toast. When I entered the kitchen she kind of jumped and looked at me. You could see the fear on her face. I said "what... why are you looking at me like that?" She said "did you see your face when you went into the bathroom?" I said "yes, I glanced at it." She said "you are really sick, aren't you?"

There was no point in lying because I had no Idea how I was going to make it back home. At this point, my hair was falling out, I could barely walk, every bone in my body hurt and I had a headache that showed no mercy. I thought I was going to die, but again this trip wasn't about me.

After I had cleaned the kitchen and sat down in the living room with her, I asked her what she wanted to do today. She said "Nothing... I don't feel too well and my legs are swollen." I said "so do you want me to clean?" This was something I always did when I went down there. She would have me clean from top to bottom, but her response caught me off guard. She said "No, I don't want you to clean. Just take it easy." So today was the Fourth of July and I asked her what she would like to eat for dinner. She said "I want a steak... a big fat T-bone and a salad!" As I write this I remember clearly, she never once told me why she wanted me to come down there.

So, our conversations began. She started talking to me about everything under the sun. She told me about all the people that had done her wrong. All the awful things my father had done to her and the way his mother and his sister had treated her. She even talked about her kids. Of course, I was excluded. I was the baby and I was perfect in her eyes. I asked her a lot of questions about the past about who she was and about her family. I regret not having a tape recorder on hand for those two days worth conversations. She told me about some of the famous people she was friends with and that she knew. She talked about her life in Mississippi and how that was the best decision she had ever made. She said she went to Mississippi to live her life and be left alone because she was always there for everyone else and now it was her turn. I told her I knew that and it was why I did not raise a big stink when she said she was moving to Mississippi and she was going to leave me in Minneapolis. I knew she was tired. I knew she struggled financially while living in Mississippi and after the divorce it was hard for me to send her money. But I managed to send her a little bit every first of the month even if it meant I had to go without. She was funny. She wanted a commitment so she wouldn't be embarrassed to ask for money each month.

Of course, by now I knew what her illness was. I had met with all her doctors on previous trips and I knew the situation, but no one had ever let on how long the situation had been going on. We even found out before she left Victoria that she was a prime candidate for Lupus. She had gotten a new rheumatologist that told her she has had Lupus for years and no one had diagnosed her. That was quite remarkable to me. But once she moved to Mississippi she never talked about it again. I recalled when I was diagnosed with Lupus. At the time, they said it was not hereditary. That was funny because at the time that my mother was diagnosed, we had 25 people on my maternal side of the family that were diagnosed with Lupus. So that blew that theory of not being hereditary out the water! Needless to say, that was the time in my life that I started really researching Lupus and working with the Lupus foundation looking for all the information I could gain on this wolf of a disease.

I could tell she was getting annoyed with me now with all my questions and I was throwing her off her daily routine. So, I told her I would go to the grocery store and get us some steaks and the makings for salads. She was more than happy to send me on my way. She had certain times of the day that she did certain things and she loved it that way. When she wanted to visit people she would go visit them and when she didn't feel well she didn't go out. She wasn't obligated to anyone with the exception of the Jehovah's Witnesses. She was loyal to the congregation. She had many friends and they thought she was one of the classiest people they had ever met. I loved them all because they loved my mom. They were the nicest group of people I had ever met. They almost had me convinced that I wanted to become a Jehovah's Witness once again in my life.

I left my mom to read her newspaper or watch her favorite television shows. Then I went on my drive around the city like I always did when I visited. I went to the park to see what festivities were going on for the holiday. I wanted to give her two or three hours alone because I knew something was up. She just wasn't telling me so I wanted to do it her way...whatever that was. I went to the car wash and lucky for me there were some nice guys there. They washed the car for me and offered up some good and funny conversation.

My last stop was to the grocery store. I had asked her if there was anything else she wanted from the store and of course she would never turn down a Pepsi. She said "bring me a case of Pepsi." That's all she wanted. When we were kids, or adults, you better not be the person to drink the last Pepsi. I returned to her apartment and she asked "Where have you been? Why have you been gone so long?" I just laughed and said "Look woman! You know you wanted me out of here so go back to your show or whatever you were doing. I'm going to fix us dinner." She said okay and laughed.

By the time dinner was complete she had moved from her bed and was back in her chair. She did not want to sit at the table, which was fine with me. All I knew was that sitting on the couch felt like I was going to be too far away from her. So, I sat on the floor right next to her chair so I could feel her legs. I was touching her legs with every movement, which ohade me feel safe. I usually don't eat a salad with my steak but I made one because she was expecting me to eat the same thing she was eating. The steak was okay to me, but she made it clear that it was the best steak she had ever had in her life! She laid her head back in the chair with the utmost look of satisfaction I had ever seen. I took her dishes to the kitchen but I chose not to clean up at that time. I just put them on the counter because I wanted to get back to my mama.

I regained my seat on the floor right beside her and as I looked at her legs and her ankles, they were huge and covered with tiny little red spots. I said "Mom! What's up with your legs?" Her response was to tell me they'd been that way for a few days. I asked if she wanted to go to the hospital. She said "No, there wouldn't be any point in that. It's a holiday and none of my doctors will be in. I don't want to deal with the ER doctors." I agreed and we continued our day talking about everything and everybody. I got a great kick out of her story about her and BB King and I kept telling her "Ma! You know you lying..." She said "If you think about it... remember whenever he was playing in Minneapolis he would always make the trip down to Victoria. He wasn't coming down to by his own records." She also made it clear that they were just great friends.

We talked about all of her brothers and sisters. My mother came from a dynamite family! We talked about recipes. She made things that no one else could make taste the way she made them. I did have my note cards ready for this conversation. Although, I pretty much got down most of her recipes since I married Arlin. My goal with Arlin was to be the perfect housewife so yes, I did learn how to cook from my mommy. There were three things that I could never quite get the hang of though. Buttermilk cornbread, cornbread dressing and sweet potato pies... Whenever those items came up for discussion I was always calling for security instructions.

I had never experienced so much joy being with my mom in all my years than in those two days. Then the conversation changed. I asked the question "Mom, what do I do if something happens to you?" She had a look of relief on her face that I brought this up. From then on, she talked nonstop about what I was supposed to do. We talked about who to call and how much money to spend. She told me to spend as little money as possible because her life insurance wasn't that big and she wanted me to have something left over.

This conversation wasn't new to us because before she left Victoria, I had drawn up her will and I was always her power of attorney. Even when she moved down south I remained her power of attorney. We just changed them up from state to state. So now I had all my instructions in hand and she seemed at peace. She never gave any indication that anything serious was wrong but we always talked about the event of death. We were never afraid to talk about death, but then the conversation changed to her obituary. She wanted it written just as she requested. I think of these things now and I kind of laugh to myself because I am the exact same way. All my instructions are clear and precise. I guess I got it from my mom. That woman was something else.

It was getting late, were both yawning and I knew it would take extra effort to get her to the doctor tomorrow. She could barely walk so I knew I'd have to push her in the wheelchair. The two of us would be a sight. Me pushing her in the wheelchair and then folding the wheelchair and putting it in the car. I asked God for the strength for tomorrow. With that prayer sleep was upon us both. We drifted off to the sound of fireworks.

Chapter 15

THE LAST MISSISSIPPI SUNSET

Morning had arrived. I looked like a scary person, but this trip wasn't about me. I told myself "keep pressing girl... Lupus is not running this show". I called moms doctor and he told me to bring her in right away. Glad we didn't have to do the emergency thing. It took her a long time to get ready. She always dressed well to go to the doctor. I get that from her as well. She always said they had more respect for you if you dressed nice and talked like you had a brain. I loved that woman! When we got there they wanted her to have a radiation treatment right away. I didn't understand that because she said she wasn't doing any treatments. Dr. Rush came down to see her and had her admitted immediately. I was getting no answers and she wasn't interested in my input. I said "...but Mom, I'm your POA." She said, "that means nothing as long as I am in my right mind!" That was my cue to shut up.

The x-rays didn't look good and they couldn't do the radiation treatment. Now I was nervous and just following along like a scared puppy dog. As I pushed the empty wheelchair I wished someone would push me. We got to her room got her all checked in and I still had no answers. It was all her business and I think she even went so far as to make the staff aware they were not to talk to me. Mama Adara wanted me to leave. She was still acting as if it was no big deal and the doctor just wanted to watch her for a day or so. I wasn't sure what to do but when my mother told me to do something I did it. She was very worried about me and wanted me in the bed. It was also bill paying time so she wanted me come back there early with bills and check book in hand. I left the wheelchair, went home, made a couple of phone calls and prayed myself to sleep... in her bed.

I woke up not realizing where I was and just laid in bed in a daze. When I realized where I was, I immediately called the hospital to talk to my mom. She answered in kind of a cheerful mood. She already had visiting her from Kingdom Hall. She told me to make sure that I brought all the things that she asked me to when I came. But, there was no rush and I could take my time. Before I let her rush me off the phone, I asked why she slept on those old mattresses when she has a new bedroom set in the guest room. She snapped! "How do you know about my mattresses?" I admitted that I slept in her bed because I wanted to be close to her. She replied" girl... you are silly. I don't know about you... I'll see you later."

I proceeded to get up and get dressed so I could make my way to the hospital, but first I had to stop by some of my favorite stores. I knew the Lupus was kicking up in a different format at this point... the dreaded bi-polar manic. I shopped all morning, buying things that I did not need but made me happy. The Lupus has taken control over my mind and body. I was spending money that I did not have and had no idea how to make it up. I remember purchasing a knee length, blue jean skirt that flared a bit. This was totally not my style. Then I purchased this giant tote bag with clocks all over it. My reasoning for the bag was to take things to mom at the hospital. I even purchased a huge painting of the magnolia flower... the manic was on. When I saw the time that was my flip back into reality. I had to get to the hospital. But first, I wanted to get back to the apartment to look at all my new purchases and try on my new skirt and fill the bag. I was completely out of my mind and I needed my therapist and my rheumatologist! I was very much out of control.

Once I made it to the hospital, I walked into my mom's room and to my relief she was alone. I still had on my little jean skirt and I couldn't wait to hear what she would have to say about it because she was very critical woman. But, to my surprise, she said it was really cute and that it looked really nice on me. I thought I would fall over dead at that moment. She didn't have anything good to say about that big giant clock bag. We set out to tend to the business at hand and talked a little. She wanted me to go to the bank, mail her bills and come right back.

Upon my return, she wanted to finish her obituary. We got bits and pieces done over the next few days. She had so much company I hardly spent any time with her. She did not want me around when she had company. I did notice she had a lot of male friends, which as I think about it, she always had lots of male friends. I think that's why my dad hated her so much. People would always come to her for advice. I learned one more thing about my mom. Because she was good friends with one of the nurses, he told me how cool my mom was and that he was blown away by the fact that she knew Jackie Robinson and went to some of his games. Nothing surprised me about her. As soon as I got the chance I asked her about Jackie Robinson and why she never told me. Her response was "...you never asked."

It was getting to be time for me to get back to Minneapolis because I was also the guardian for my brother. I needed to take care of his monthly business as well. I happened to get to the hospital early enough in the day that I got to talk to her doctor. He said that she was being bothered by a lot of lymph nodes again and they needed to see if they could go in and help her out. They were trying to get a line in but her veins were collapsing. The next day when I went in she was black and blue from them trying to get this line in so they decided to send her down to surgery and have a surgeon put it in. They said it would be a quick procedure and she would be back in the room within the hour.

Dr. Rush returned to the room and was astonished at the bruising, but he said after they get the line in he could get her fixed up by giving her blood. My mom was pretty out of it by now, but she woke up real fast to say no blood! Dr. Rush remembered that she was a Jehovah's Witness and they would not do blood transfusions under any circumstances. I knew this because she always made that very clear. Dr. Rush called me into the hall and asked if I was going along with this decision because he knew I had the power to override her at this point. I told him I would honor her wish because if I didn't and she woke up, she would never speak to me again after she slapped me. They came to get her to see if they could get a line in and she instructed me to do a few things and come right back. I said okay crazy lady. I'm going and I'll be right back. I kissed her bye.

I returned in about 40 minutes and was directed to the surgical area where she was. I went and checked and they told me a little while longer. I waited nearly an hour and asked them to check on her again. The phone rang and I knew it was for me. It was the surgeon. She said the good news was they got the line in, but her heart was shutting down. She was having heart failure and/or a heart attract. She instructed me to go to her room and she would be on her way. Now I was in panic mode, running through the hallways of the hospital not knowing what to expect. Her room was right outside of a waiting area so I parked myself there and started making phone calls. Then I looked up to see a group of nurses running with her and her favorite nurse was straddling her in the bed. They were trying to get her stable so she could see me. He said she had been calling for me and she wanted to be back in her room with me. I was still not thinking death until Dr. Rush returned and asked me one more time about blood and the do not resuscitate order. I had to go with her wishes no matter how much it hurt because this was not about me. I asked how long she had. When he said "maybe thirty minutes" I nearly passed out. He was also very complimentary about my mom. He said when she came to Mississippi she already had lymphoma and had outlived his prediction by five years.

I went back to my mom because she was calling me. I said "mom I'm here." She said "Adele... Adele, I love you." At first, I was in the room alone with her but when she started to choke and I didn't know what to do. So, her favorite nurse came in and sat in the back of the room and talked me through the transition. She wanted water so I tried to give it to her but she couldn't take it. The nurse Derick asked me if I wanted to get in the bed. I said "no, just let the rails down so I could be close". I asked her if she wanted me to brush her hair, and she mouthed yes." She had such beautiful hair and I brushed and brushed all while she kept saying my name. I know she was so scared of leaving me alone since Arlin was no longer in my life. I finally mustered up the courage to let her go. As I was brushing her hair, I said "mama it's okay, your work is done here... it's time for you to rest. I will be okay, we will be okay. I love you." Then she started reaching for the light. I looked at Derick the nurse and he said" she reached for the light of transition." After a short while and a few more brush strokes she closed her eyes and peace was upon her. July 12, 2002, I lost a part of me that I knew I would never ever get back. My mom, Adara Abel, left me.

Derick asked me to go into the waiting area while they cleaned her up and I could come back in and sit with her and brush her hair. While waiting I made the phone calls until I got tired of telling the story. I went back in and sat almost with no emotion. There was nothing else to be said. Then the funeral home arrived so I left the room. I had never felt so empty when they wheeled her away. I went back to the room to gather her belongings and once again I sat in that waiting area. I thought about what to do next. I was in Mississippi all alone and pretty much in this world all alone. A couple guys were going to the elevator. They were visiting in the next room so they knew what was going on. They asked if anyone was coming and I said no so they insisted that I let them help me get the stuff to my car.

After a few hours, I finally made it back to mama Adara's home. I just sat in her chair thinking of all the things I had to do. I would do it because this trip was not about me and my Lupus. News spread fast and family was on the way. The biggest surprise and comfort was that Arlin was on the next plane out. Oh, how I needed him! I sat in that chair for a couple of days, thinking about moms wishes and knowing I had to have two services. One in Mississippi and one in Victoria where she would be laid to rest. Everything else was a blur, but my trip was clear and I knew for sure it wasn't about me. I had always made everything about me. I let Lupus run my life, but not this time. I wore my big girl panties.

I told this long story to show that Lupus does not care about anything or anyone. When dealing with this disease you have to always keep a solid perspective. After all the emotions of my trip were put into place, the Lupus let loose! Everything that could go wrong went wrong. The kidney disease was getting worse, the discussion of dialysis came up, my vision was going bad and my heart had decided to get in on the action. My skin was turning all shades of black with three different types of rashes plaguing me at the same time. Walking was almost impossible. My mental state was declining to the point that my therapist came to my home. This was one of those times that my life was on the line.

Finally, the hospital became my home for a while. The doctors were not sure what to do for me. It was now time for chemotherapy to come into play. It was something new they were trying out because it had worked in some cases. That Lupus flare lasted nearly a year. When you talk about Lupus you have to include the depression that goes along with it. I experienced a major Lupus flare, Lupus depression led by manic episodes and the grieving process of losing my mother. Lupus will exacerbate anything and make life twice as difficult. While I was still in Mississippi and family and friends were there, I was still taking care of the business at hand and no one knew or acknowledged what I was going through. If you wonder how I did it, it was my manic-depressive disorder that got me through. I was on a high for two weeks in order to take care of my mom. I broke down from grief a month later, when I cried for the first time.

Chapter 16

CHEMO AND THE MOTORCYCLE

Moving from my house, giving up my dog, losing my mom and the divorce proved to be so stressful that the Lupus exacerbated into the need for chemotherapy. I was sure my time was up. When diagnosed I was given a ten-year survival rate; however, I had kicked that prediction in the butt! I had gone through a lot, always sick, people telling it was in my head and I couldn't wait for this wolf to take me out.

This time I felt happy at the thought of dying. My mom had left me and I wanted nothing more than to be with her. The chemo was nothing nice. I couldn't function at all. One day it seemed I woke up and I was nearly 100 pounds lighter. I tried on my favorite black dress that I purchased when I first got sick and lost a ton of weight. My word... it fit! Suddenly I didn't want to stay in the bed any longer. I had the will and determination to do something I always wanted to do... get my motorcycle license and get a bike! Everyone was riding, even my son. My daughter Adara decided she wanted to take a class. My ex-husband had been riding for years and I always wanted to ride with him.

Adara and I agreed to take a class together. She was so worried about me, but her attitude was if that makes mommy happy, go for it. We went through the classroom portion with no problem, though it was a fight to stay awake. I was somewhat embarrassed about my age. We took our test and got our temps. But actually riding was a chore for me. Back in the day when Arlin tried to teach me to ride, I was so scary and had no balance. The instructor was a butt head and he was always yelling at me. Rightfully so because I could barely hold the bike up and it was only a two hundred pounder! We were going through an obstacle course. First, I fell then I kept hitting the cones. All these young kids, mostly males, got a good laugh out of me.

And the mean instructor said, "if you can't get through this you will flunk!" I replied, "I know!" At which time the whole class laughed. Finally my Adara stood in the middle of the group and yelled at everyone. "This is my mom and I don't see anyone else's mom out here trying to live her dream while going through chemotherapy! She has trouble holding up the bike because she's too weak. Now I suggest you shut the hell up!" The instructor came up to me and apologized and said he would help me any way he could. Then asked why I was doing this. With a smile I told him "they say my time is coming to an end and I want to accomplish something I always wanted to do but was too afraid." He said "ok, but you have to get through this obstacle course before I can pass you."

It was my turn and of course now all eyes were on me. "Adele you're up" called the instructor from the other end. I said, "yes sir and I'm on my way!" That was the longest two minutes of my life! I knew I had to do it because I knew I would never try again. I took off like I was evil Knievel, running straight lines, missing every cone in my path, doing circles and running that course like I was the instructor! The end was near and so was I! I passed like a champ to the hoorays of the other students. I was more proud of my daughter for standing up for me. I couldn't let her down. The instructor handed me my waiver and after class we headed straight to department of motor vehicles. I was now licensed!

Now to get a bike. I happened to have an extra car around that I had no need for. My time was drawing to a close and another family member needed a car. I decided to sell it for blue book value and my dream was there for the taking. Money in hand... motorcycle shop here I come! I summoned my son Bennett to drive me out there. I didn't have the energy to drive let alone ride a motorcycle. I did not care what my mind was set on going to get it today. Bennett was all for it. His thought process was that I couldn't ride whatever I chose, which meant he had another bike to ride. My selfish child was a lot like me. The store was quite a ways away but it was well worth the trip. I stepped in the door and my heart melted like butter. So many beautiful machines to choose from with every color under the rainbow. I had no idea what I was looking for. I just figured something would catch my eye. Something glistening with purple because that was my favorite color.

I stopped and looked no further! Black, silver and purple... done looking... now let's talk. I chose a beautiful Victory 1000. Yes this was the manic kicking in, but I didn't care. When the manic kicked in there was very little to talk about and no changing my mind. My son Bennett had little to say. "If that's what you want... get it." I started negotiating with my salesman, Rick, who by the way was so good looking I could envision myself riding on the back of his red Harley that he had pointed out to me. After a bit of haggling, we reached a very reasonable price. Rick didn't know he was dealing with a well-trained negotiator with cash in hand. Once I let my skills be known, he was willing to play ball. We haggled down to the last fifty dollars, a new helmet and gloves. I was kind of disappointed this interaction had come to an end. I had such a good time!

My son Bennett just stood by quietly, knowing there was nothing he could say or do. He knew my groove, although I don't think he realized it was the bi-polar and the chemo leading me on this wild ride. I kept up such a ruckus that everyone in the store was like a part of my comedic song and dance. The time had come. We closed the deal and he asked if I was riding it back. He had no idea I was scared to death. I played the game so well, he never even asked how long I had been riding for fear of insulting me. So calmly I said, "no I'll pick it up tomorrow with my husband Arlin Hamilton." He hesitated then asked, "The Police Chief?" I said, "yep that's him." They knew Arlin very well. He didn't need to know he was my ex-husband.

I finally tied Arlin down to get him to go check out the bike and whether or not I got a good deal. More importantly, I needed him to ride the damn thing back to the city for me! It was an uncomfortable ride with Arlin because our divorce was weird. We never spoke ill of one another. We always just greeted each other with a hug and a kiss. We didn't have much of a conversation unless it concerned the kids. Finally, my prize was home and safely stored in my garage. During the ride, Arlin did commit to teaching me to ride one on one. With a deep hug and kiss we said our goodbyes until tomorrow.

I fell into bed from exhaustion from the day's chemo treatment and another long ride to and from the bike shop. I had to muster up more energy to drive myself back home, while Arlin had a blast riding my new toy back to the city. I was satisfied and very pleased that Arlin was impressed with my purchase.

I woke up feeling kind of let down and depressed because the fun of the hunt was over. I was no longer on that manic high and now I wished for death again. I was looking for an excuse to get out of this morning's chemo treatment because it was so depressing. Watching all those people sitting around with bags attached, with the hope of beating cancer and gently smiling at each other was hard. Then there was me. The lucky one without cancer, but suffering from a flare of Lupus that I wished was cancer. I always went alone because I didn't want anyone feeling sorry for me. That always back fired because I usually ended up feeling sorry for myself.

After treatment, I slowly rushed home, knowing Arlin said he would meet me there for a lesson. To my surprise he was only thirty minutes late. I could not get excited, but I needed to go through with it to show my family this wasn't just another one of buying sprees. This was all that it really was. I could care less about that bike now. Lesson one was to ride down the road slowly, turn around and return. Next up... ride to a vacant lot where a box store is going up. Ride around for a bit and return home. Then, ride down the road and turn around. It was so far so good until I looked up and saw a group of three or four extremely good looking young men all dressed in white. I forgot what I was doing and down I went. These guys came running over to me. I was thinking "dam why was Arlin here?" He was there in jiffy and it was him that picked me up. At that point, I promised myself if I fell three times that bike was history. Arlin put the bike up after I took many pictures on it.

The next day Arlin didn't show up, so I decided I could do this myself. My treatment had gone okay. My daughter Abella and her brother Bryce came by as I was taking the bike out. They looked a bit worried but said nothing. I took more pictures and finally Bryce said, "well are you going to ride it or just take pictures?" That little shit head pissed me off, so I dressed in my gear and started it up and proceeded down the driveway. I think maybe I got 100 yards and down I went! That big bike was lying right on top of me and I was hurt. After my kids picked up the bike, it was evident I was banged up. They made me go to the hospital. Since it was a holiday, I had to have my chemo treatment in the emergency room. So, I figured it would be funny to return there. When they saw me, they thought something was seriously wrong until I told them why I was there. They did not think it was so funny that I was trying to ride a motorcycle. They even called my doctor on me! He gave direct orders that I was never to ride again if I was in treatment. They bandaged me up and sent me home to bed.

I arrived home and the whole family was there including Arlin. The girls always called their dad when something was wrong with me. After the long lecture, they put me to bed and all left for a holiday cookout at their dads. This was fall number two. I didn't have treatment the next day, but I felt bad... real bad. I made a quick run to the grocery store just to get some fruit. I had been so weak I was drinking ensure on a regular basis. I got in line behind these two old women, I think they were sisters, they talked and talked, then argued.

I could feel myself getting sick so I asked the ladies if I could please get by. They ignored me or maybe they couldn't hear me. There was a guy in line behind me and he could tell something was wrong when I dropped my fruit. He asked, "what you need?" I said, "I just need to get through and get to the bathroom." In this loud booming voice, he said "ladies can you please move and let this woman through." Just as he said, 'she's sick', at least a gallon of chocolate ensure pour from my mouth all over these two women! Of course, the rescue squad was in route. As I was being rolled out, I saw that gentleman with wads of paper towels cleaning up my mess. I never got to thank him. As I was being put into the squad I felt better. I think it was just all that ensure. I drove myself home, pulled into the garage and there sat my world wind purchase which meant nothing to me. I think that's what drove me to my final ride on the purple beauty.

I figured that if I was meant to have this bike, I should be able to ride it. SOOOOOOOOOOOO I pulled the bike out. Up and down the drive way, nice turns, wind blowing in my hair... I am doing this! I take my baby to the street, the whole block, corners sharp and good. Then I started to feel bad again, so I headed back to the garage. I pull up and get off the bike while I wait for the door to open. I got back on the bike and slowly rolled it into its spot. As I got there, down I go! Fall number 3. Three strikes and I was out. Was I sad? Absolutely not! I already had my eye on a very expensive sofa! I did become the laughing stock of the family though. I kept getting calls asking if I had fallen off the couch yet.

Chapter 17

MY EVERYDAY SUPERMAN

I was born the youngest of three siblings. There were quite a few years between me and the other two. I was very close to my brother Torin, but not so close my sister Olivia. I worshipped the ground my brother walked on and rightfully so. He was a Vietnam Veteran who proudly served with The United States Marine Corps. I was young when he went into the service and didn't even understand that there was a war going on. I do remember he was always the one in the neighborhood that fought all the time and was always getting into trouble with his friends. I do remember my parents hoping he would enlist in the service because they figured it would do him some good. He enlisted under the buddy system with his best friend.

One night, very late... the phone rang. I could hear my mother telling my father that it was a call from Korea. When it got quiet I wondered if Torin was dead. I was sitting in the middle of my bed looking around my room. It used to be Torin's room, but when I got the room my mom and I redecorated and everything was purple or lilac. Purple was both mine and Torin's favorite color. My mom walked by and I yelled to find out what happened. She looked rattled but calmly said "your brother was injured in the war and he is now heading to Japan. He will eventually be heading home to begin the healing process of what he went through for our country." After studying about that war, I was so angry at how our soldiers were treated. I always hoped that Torin would talk about the experience but he never did to me.

I have included my brother in my journey because he was a big part of it. Soon after being out of the service he turned to drugs.

Apparently, drugs were always available to him and his buddies at war, so it was natural that the desire would follow him home. He soon was declared 100 percent disabled and of course issued the Purple Heart. A few years later, the courts found him incompetent to care for himself so an attorney was granted for him to handle his finances. Torin's drug habit was so bad the attorney withdrew and I became his court ordered guardian of his person and finances. I was his caregiver for thirty-five years. That thirty-five years included my life with Lupus and a strained marriage.

He eventually got clean and stayed clean for nearly twenty years of his life. Torin's body paid a hefty price because of the many years of drug use. This meant, while I was taking care of me, I also had to take care of him. This was a major burden over the past ten years because he had as many doctors as I did and his appointments outnumbered mine. I took him to his appointments and managed all his affairs. We would joke about which one of us would go first because the last ten years we both had been so ill. The stress was overwhelming at times. There were a number of occasions where we both were hospitalized at the same time. Torin would be at Veterans Administration Hospital and I would be at University of Minnesota and Medical College Hospital. I would have to check myself out to go to the VA to sign for a procedure for him and then go and be readmitted to my hospital.

My doctors kept urging me to give him up and put him into a facility, but I just couldn't do that. He still had life in him. He had a girlfriend and they still did things together. His children had finally found it bearable and safe to have a relationship with him. They'd had a very difficult time dealing with their father the drug addict, but once he was clean and sober they got to finally know the sweet and gentle guy he was. He lived with me on more than one occasion. There was a time when I went to live with Adara and he came along because it was easier for her to look after both of us in one household. We were kind of the joke of the neighborhood because the rescue squad would come for one of us at least two times a week. The neighbors would take bets on whether it was Torin or me.

He made me sick and I made him sick because we were so worried about one another. The stress was killing us both. He fell a lot and when he would fall the entire house would shake. I would have a panic attack behind him falling and that's how we would end up in in the hospital at the same time. Lupus appeared to be in a quiet remission and I was getting around slowly but surely. I had no idea that mean-spirited Lupus was just lying in wait. Then suddenly, out of nowhere, I had a massive stroke and a bad heart attack. If nothing else is taken from my story, believe me when I say, stress is real and it has to be kept under control.

My brother was well enough that I thought I would give him one last shot at independence. I got him and apartment next door to me. That boy worked my nerves but I loved him and would do anything for him. He had tears flowing when I took him to his new home. Everything was done and in place. All he had to do was walk in and sit down. I had never seen Torin so happy. One year he kept saying "I can't believe this is my place" and then his body started deteriorating rapidly. Finally, it was clear he could no longer live alone. The fight was on because he refused to go into a nursing home. The Marine in his blood told him he was okay and he could take of himself. Needless to say, I won. I found a wonderful rehab and nursing home he loved. After rehab, he was placed there permanently. Torin lived good there for a year before his kidneys went on a rapid shut down pace. They failed because of medicines he took for his mental health. He was tired but I was glad he left this world before I did. I always worried who would take care of him if I wasn't here.

All the running back and forth across town to the nursing home and to the VA had finally come to an end. My brother was very smart and wise and I learned a lot from him. I dubbed him my purple rose. We sent him off with military honors on a sunny afternoon. Once again, I was interrupted by Lupus. In order to bury him I had to check myself out of the hospital and immediately following the service, I had to head right back in. This episode of Lupus centered on bleeding issues. My counts were low and it seemed I was bleeding from everywhere. I had to attend the service with my face bandaged up.

I saved some of his ashes and had them placed in a beautiful purple rose. Torin sits on my desk overseeing my story. Healed from my latest bout of unbearable pain, I went to bed for two months. During that time, my body did heal and I remember our conversations about me writing some kind of book. I swear I could hear Torin's quiet voice saying "now is the time to do something for you. I'm good and you're free to take care of you and do what you want." In that moment, my purpose had begun to be revealed to me. I would share my story in hopes to enlighten someone else about the struggles of Lupus because my struggle wasn't normal. By the third month following my brothers passing, I was back up and getting myself into my groove. It was no one else's... just mine and I formulated a plan to fulfill my purpose.

Chapter 18

MY HEART ATTACKED ME

I had recently moved into my daughter Adara's house. I had been previously living in my condo, but her trips across town were becoming too time-consuming. I had been in this Lupus flare for approximately 6 months and something was always wrong. I found myself calling on my children constantly. I knew I was becoming a major burden to them, so when Adara suggested I come and live with her because it would be easier for her to take care of me. I reluctantly agreed.

Things were going okay. I was still up and around, driving myself to doctors' appointments and wherever else I needed to go. On occasion, I did do a shopping spree, but it was one of the few times that I had free money. I wasn't spending money I didn't have. All my bills were being paid. I had fun redecorating Adara's house. My flare for the eclectic decorating style was still there. I even found myself cooking for change. I hadn't done that for a while because when the Lupus ran my life, I did little to nothing.

Before I knew it, I became the paramedic's new number one patient. They knew me by name. They came for me for so many different reasons. My kidneys caused me a lot of pain they and they were shutting down again. They also came because there were times that I could not walk or function at all. What was so peculiar about this Lupus flare was that, one day I would be up doing community healthcare fairs and speaking on Lupus and then there were other days I couldn't speak. I couldn't think... I just felt as if I was losing my mind. This is how the Lupus would hit me with no rhyme or reason. I will go to the hospital and they didn't know what to do with me. My blood levels were off, simply signifying that I was in the

Lupus flare.

When I didn't think things could get any worse all of a sudden, I had a horrible Lupus attack and found myself suddenly sliding down the back of my dog. Adara had a big, old English Sheep dog. He was my baby and he was always in the room with me. He was my bodyguard...I so miss Buddy. This particular day in February seemed fine and I was doing okay. I was taking my time getting dressed and Buddy sat watching me. Normally he would be laying down with his eyes on me. I remember looking at him and asking what he was looking at and he just stared at me, of course. Suddenly I felt funny... nothing seemed to be moving and I couldn't speak. I felt my body sliding down and Buddy had positioned himself between me and the bed and I could feel his silky fir on my legs. Then, I was on the floor, laid out, staring into space. I could hear sounds of Buddy jumping up and down on the hallway floor. Apparently, he was trying to get Adara's' attention. I had not made any noise in route to the floor because I had slid down Buddy's' back. I could hear Adara and her friend talking in the living room and finally Adara acknowledged Buddy because he was making so much noise, which was not his norm.

Finally, she came to see what his problem was and found me on the floor. I was too big for her to lift me back into bed so I laid there thinking something was wrong and I needed help. But, I couldn't relay that to her and her friend. I just remember laying there with only a shirt on and no pants, wishing I could get up. Adara called my cousin Deloren and asked what to do. Deloren said call 911! After making the call, Adara realized I didn't have any pants on and asked me if I wanted pants on. Then she proceeded to go through my closet looking for the right outfit. Her friend told her to just put some sweat pants on me. It was the weirdest feeling to be aware of everything going on around you but unable to speak. Buddy stayed right beside me until the paramedics arrived. No one even had to tell him to go downstairs. One of the firemen caught a glimpse of him leaving and he was like... "Wholly shit! Did you see that dog?" His partner said "yes and I was glad he was going out the door." I heard someone ask if the dog was locked up. It was so weird hearing all the commotion going on and all I could do was stare into space and say nothing.

They determined I was having a stroke and immediately

nothing mattered but getting me to the hospital. I remember looking out trying to figure what route they were taking and that was the last thing I remembered for a long time. I was told the doctors were looking for a time frame to determine if I was still eligible for the medicine that could reduce the effects of a stoke. Apparently, I was. Thank you Lord!

I woke up in ICU to my family staring at me and wondering if this was it. When I opened my eyes I was immediately pissed that all these people were here looking at me! Even Arlin was standing in the background. I hated anyone to know what I was going through. Of course I was grateful that I even woke up because I wasn't supposed to. I had a massive stroke and a serious heart attack as a side order. I think this disease they call Lupus is something of another world. It is so strange and mysterious...just like the wolf they compare it to. I say that because I was up and back at home in five days. How does that happen? I was walking and talking, had regained 85 to 90 percent of my functions, and was going to rehab. That only lasted for a short period.

I became so depressed during this time that it was so evident that my cousin Deloren started coming around more often. Deloren was one of the few people I let near me. I was very private as far as my family was concerned with the Lupus. I really didn't want anyone seeing me like this, family or friends. I think my cousin had a feeling that I was going into a very deep depression and that's why she was around more often than I would have liked her to be. Deloren was always in my face like... "do you need this, is there something I can for you, what's the matter, what are you feeling...?" She drove me crazy!

One day she decided to get me out of the house. She knew how much I loved driving my car, but she hated it because it was a stick shift and she couldn't drive me around. When I drove my car, which was a five speed, it was the only time I felt in control. There was just something about shifting those gears that gave me a certain power... a power I can't explain. To this day I miss my car and I'm mad at my son Bennett for taking it away from me. He said I was too sick to drive anymore.

I remember in the hospital they had talked about me going to a nursing home, but in my mind that was never happening. I remember when my mother was in her final crisis. They wanted her to go to a nursing home just for a few days while I came home to care for my brother. She was having none of that! As a matter of fact, before she went into the hospital we talked about nursing homes in general. She said she would die before she would go. My mama lived and died true to her word. That was my feeling as well. I was either going to get through this trauma or find a way to die. I had many plans in my arsenal. I guess the Lord was not quite ready for this pig-headed lady named Adele Bijour.

Chapter 19

ALL WILL TO LIVE, WAS GONE UNTIL........

Following the stroke and heart attack I returned to live with Adara... if you could call it living. I was so depressed and now my depression consisted of absolute sadness. Thought of taking my life had passed. I remember just lying in bed watching television day and night. Sometimes I ventured out to the front porch to watch the goof balls on the block. I was so embarrassed about how I looked. I remember I had a friend who thought I was the prize of a lifetime when I was in my good years. I was working out daily and enjoying life for the first time in years.

He came by to see me because my best friend in the world had passed away and I wanted him to render a drawing of her. I cringed when he came in. He said "Ooh! Times must be tough. You moved from the condo to the hood and you look like death! Wow! I can't believe how fat you are! What happened to you?" I can't even believe I went through with the order. My feelings were so hurt. I died right then. I finally told him I had a stroke and a heart attack. His response was "that's is too bad." That meeting sent me spiraling down.

I was already struggling with the fact that my best friend had died. She went through a load of her own medical issues. We hung in there together. We were best friends since we met at Chanhassen High School and I could never imagine my life without her. We both feared who would go first. She worried about me to the point that she would be in the hospital and would have to talk to me in case something happened. She didn't understand Lupus and really didn't want to know. She just didn't want me sick. The divorce really bothered her. Our husbands were close friends, but she held strong that her husband could never have socialized with Arlin and any other women.

She was funny. She said we were friends first and introduced the two jackasses to each other. I will say that kind of went the same way for me. She wanted to know what was going on in my life, but she never wanted me to bring another man around. I was so angry that night. Bennett was with his dad when Craig called to say Theresa has passed away, Arlin wouldn't even come and tell me. He told Bennett to "go tell your mama". Again, I was left all alone to deal with my pain. God please take me too! I managed to make it to the funeral, but I ran out as soon as it was over. All I ever had was my mother and Theresa. I was just a bowl of Jell-O® with no color.

I started taking medicine just to sleep and never got dressed, except to go to the doctor. I cried every time I saw that stupid wheel chair. Now I had oxygen because the Lupus was affecting my lungs. How much more Lord? I hated everything and everyone. I got so mad when Adara's friends would step in to say hi. I would just take more pills. I thought the Lupus was in remission because I wasn't in any pain. No rashes, not feeling ill, just feeling nothing. Well I found out that nothing was the Lupus silently targeting my lungs.

Abella started coming by more often and I would notice her and Adara whispering. Finally, Abella came and laid on the bed with me. Adara stood at the door as if she was there for support. My brother was sitting there as well. He was always listening. Abella finally spit it out.

"Mom... I'm pregnant." Before I could respond my big eared brother yells,

"You gonna have a baby? Awe that's great." End of discussion. Abella is the last one I would expect to have a baby. So, I was positive it was not on purpose. Accidents happen.

"You aren't going to say anything?" she asked

"No... wait... we're having a baby, right?" I replied

"I wouldn't do anything different." I noticed with every

question she had for me I became a little more alive.

Then Adara decided she wanted to move in with her boyfriend and suggested Abella move in and take the upper level. Once Abella moved in I started moving around a bit more and my brother Torin started asking me to cook. I started cooking and a little cleaning and waiting for Abella's next question. Now there was no way I wanted to be anywhere but here. The major drawback to me cooking was I couldn't remember how to cook much. So, they were joyful when my sister would come over to cook. It seemed the only thing I could remember how to cook was barbeque chicken in the oven and brownies. Torin and Abella would just cringe at the thought. I don't think they realized that I lost memory after the stroke.

I was working hard at regaining all the functions I had lost due to the stroke. I do know the best $800.00 I ever spent was on the iPad. Before the stroke I was pretty good with the computer, but I had to start from scratch. It took time but I soon got it. It was now getting closer to the baby. I was doing so well we thought maybe I could babysit. We got the living quarters set up and had a cool baby shower, thanks to Scotty. For some reason, Abella had to have a five-hundred dollar baby bed! I told her that was between her and her dad. I guess they worked it out because she got the bed. Everything was in place and she worked right up to delivery. Abella came down and told me she didn't feel well and that the pain was coming every few minutes. I said "ok let's time it, ten minutes apart, let's go!" I took her to the hospital! I called her dad and of course he was on his way. It wasn't long before my life entered this world. MiaBella Imani had arrived!

We learned day one after the six weeks had passed... I wasn't the babysitter. I wasn't well enough. What I did get to experience was every night when Abella would come in from work she would lay my princess on my chest. There was no better medicine than feeling that little heart beat on my chest. I waited all day for those few minutes. Sometimes it was longer if she didn't cry. This was my life saver. I had been saved so many times, but this was the best.

After a few months, Abella decided to get an apartment on her own. This was perfect timing for Bennett because his most recent romance had bit the dust so he would gladly move back in. Besides, it was his house to begin with. Abella said, "mom you have to get up and get out of here and try to live on your own. You need quiet." She said we could put me into low income housing where there would be just enough room for me. So, now my wheels were turning. What would I do about Torin? Bennett was saying he needed a part time job. I found out that Torin qualified for personal care that would all be paid for by the Veterans Administration because he was 100% disabled. So, I offered Bennett the job of being Torin's care giver. The proposition was good and Bennett agreed. That meant I could move out and not worry about Torin's day to day care.

I felt as if I had been given new life! I chose an apartment out of the city but still close. Abella and I moved within days of one another. I was liberated! The place was small but it would do. My neighbors were an interesting group and they were infatuated with me. Some of them had never been around people of color so they were curious. I tried to keep to myself but these folks were persistent! I really didn't care because I was starting over. Shopping had reentered my life! If I thought this is where my Lupus problems ended, I was wrong.

Chapter 20

ANOTHER DIAGNOSIS

As I was laying down waiting to die after the heart attack and stroke, I again realized that God wasn't having any of that. It was time to start moving around. I was still unable to walk on my own and my body now required oxygen 24/7. My fight was just beginning. I thought Lupus had given me enough, but boy was I wrong! I cried for days when the guy came to deliver my motorized wheel chair. Now when people saw me they finally realized I was indeed sick. Before the chair and oxygen I looked fine. That's a real tear jerker when people say you look fine to me. It insinuated I was just lazy. My weight would vary from heavy to small so the assumption was that I just needed to work harder with my weight so I could stay small.

At first, I didn't understand why I needed the chair. I just assumed, like everyone else, I was out breath because I was overweight. I could not walk from my bedroom to the living room. I was really focused on getting out of that wheel chair. It was getting bad. But, then I thought, maybe I'd just make good use of the chair and people would stop judging me. I decided what I needed was a wheelchair assessable van. The wheels of my mind started ticking as I tried to figure out how I could get one. I started applying to different agencies and even tried to put on a fund raiser for myself. Suddenly I realized I was just making myself even more disabled. I stopped all those thoughts and started a new process because I hated how that made me look. I was not going down like that. I knew it was going to be a long process.

By this time in my life I would not see very many people. I pretty much stopped going to church because it was just too hard.

Then one day my Pastor and his wife said they were coming over and not taking no for an answer. You don't tell the Pastor no. He had been watching over me since my divorce. We had a nice little chit chat and he was still laughing about a video he had seen on the internet. So, we pulled it up and all had the greatest laugh. I realized he was looking at me as a child of God and the storms I had been through were just that... storms and storms passed. We prayed and he said they would be back. No pressure whatsoever. That was my wake-up call. I decided I was getting out of that chair.

Dr. Anderson referred me to a pulmonologist for my breathing issues. I was fighting pneumonia on a regular basis and he knew there was more to the pneumonia. I saw the first pulmonologist and after the first visit and lots of testing, she referred me to Dr. Benson. I asked if I had done something wrong because I always took pride in treating my team of doctors with the utmost respect. She laughed and said that unfortunately my case was quite severe and Dr. Benson was one of the best in the world. She said I should count myself lucky that I got him. I saw him the next day and after reviewing my test results he was glad I was in. He admitted me for more testing and by the time I was discharged he had given me the diagnoses of pulmonary embolism, pulmonary fibrosis and Pulmonary Hypertension.

Apparently, my case was so severe that I was referred to a doctor who was not even taking on any new patients. He was so highly regarded that people came from all over the country to see him. After a lot of testing and procedures he was not pleased to tell me I had this disease and there was no cure. He confirmed that it was brought on because of the Lupus. I could tell he really cared and he could see the confusion in my eyes. He tried to explain this disease but I did not have a clue. Finally, I just asked the question...

"How long do I have?" "

"Around five years."

"Did the Lupus really caused this?"

"Yes, and your heart is very involved from the heart attack and stroke." I was just speechless. Here I was trying to pump myself up from my latest depression and trying to get on with my life. Now, I was again wondering how much more I could take. Again, a weird disease with no cure and very difficult to explain... just no words. I had felt alone all my life, but nothing like now. Damn, just damn!

Pulmonary Arterial Hypertension is also a disease that is often misdiagnosed like Lupus. This time I was lucky because I had one of the best PH doctors in the world and he knew what he was looking for. This is often referred to as PH or PAH. The first information I received was high blood pressure in my lungs. I had never heard of such a thing! The two are unrelated. The other type of high blood pressure is another animal. I also learned that without aggressive treatment this disease was fatal. Great news on this snowy Monday. This was going to be yet another process.

I was immediately put on medications for this trouble maker of a disease. I went back in one month to find no improvement. He wanted to get very aggressive with my treatment. That meant running a line in my chest to pump medication into my body 24/7. This is known as something called remodulin. I would have to wear a pump on my body all the time and refill the pump every 48 hours. This was so serious that I would have to be admitted to ICU for five days so my body could get used to it. He explained the headaches would be nothing I had ever experienced. It was going to be awful! So, he gave me a few days to think about. In the meantime, I saw a new cardiologist who wanted to put a pacemaker in because my heart wasn't doing what it was supposed to. While Dr. Benson was waiting for my decision, he wanted one more procedure done.

This frog on my back often felt like I was dying because I couldn't breathe. Chest pain was a regular visitor and I was always dizzy. I couldn't do anything in a hurry. I had a persistent cough, sometimes swollen feet and ankles and of course the mainstream ride of chronic fatigue. Let me not forget to mention there was fainting for no reason at all. The heart is tied into all this. When pressure in the lungs increases, the heart has to work harder. I think one of the worse feelings was when I was lying down and I couldn't breathe, even with oxygen. I never knew when that last breath would be.

So, I had the pacemaker put in. No problem. Then came the

test Dr. Benson wanted done as soon as possible. I agreed to that and went in for the routine procedure. Little did I know that nothing is routine with Ms. Adele. Dr. Benson wanted my answer now! So, I gave my consent to go on the medication, but before I could go in to get it started, there was a little problem with my routine procedure. The doctor that performed the procedure nicked a vein. I came home from the procedure for the second day and by now I could no longer walk. The pain was off the charts! I called Dr. Anderson and his office said to come in for an ultra sound. I had my son Bennett take me in. He was in a hurry because he and his friends were off on a weekend motorcycle trip. Once the ultra sound started, I knew I was in trouble when the tech just ran out of the room. She didn't even close the door!

Some doctor came in and said they could fix in a minor procedure, but I would have to go some lab I had never heard of on the lower level. They wheeled me back to the waiting area and said someone would come and get me. Everyone was in a hurry to leave because it was Friday evening. No one seemed to be paying me much attention. Bennett looked at me with that look and then he asked how much longer it was going to take. I was a bit hurt and irritated so I found the doctor and asked how long. She implied it was nothing and maybe an hour. So, I told Bennett to go ahead and go I would get a ride. Abella would be getting off work soon and I'd just ask her to come and get me. Finally, someone came to take me back in for the procedure. I was concerned as to how Abella was going to find me when it was time to be picked up. They took me to a place I had never been in The University Hospital. I thought I had been everywhere. I even knew where the morgue was!

Now I was in no-man's land... waiting. Finally, the staff down there wheeled me in, looked at me and the ultra sound and said there was no way they could do this. They told me I needed full emergency surgery! Now I'm shaking out of control. They wheeled me in a big hurry to another place. Finally, I was able to speak to someone and I asked what was wrong. I was bleeding internally bleeding and it was bad. I was pretty sure I was dying at this point. Everyone was moving so fast, yet they were calm. I guess that's the training. I thought about my kids. They prepped for surgery and told me Abella was there and asked if I wanted to see her. Of course, I whispered. I could tell my body was making preparations.

Abella came in with MiaBella. I could not speak at that point. So, I couldn't bark my orders. I could only think of Adara, Bennett and Bryce. I wouldn't get a chance to say bye. Then they rushed me away. I was out before they gave me anything. I woke in ICU to the doctor telling me he fixed it, but I had lost so much blood the transfusions needed to continue.

I remember laying there and the sister nurse was in a pissed off mood for whatever reason. She was mad because they attached little bags to catch the blood and monitor it. I remember her just cussing... spewing fire at me! Those bags were filling fast. As soon as she would clean up the mess I would be over flowing again. It was as if the blood they were giving me was pouring straight through. She finally got the doctor back and he didn't want to admit he was unsuccessful the first time, so he wanted to wait it out. I still couldn't talk. My head was just spinning and I was thinking no one should have to die like this. Then a while later the nurse from hell started yelling. "Somebody needs to do something and fast! This woman is dying and the blood is not slowing down!" Finally, the surgeon came back and said "yes, we have to go back in. Get her prepped." I was thinking there was no way I was going to make it. I was a high risk for surgery and to be put all the way under. There was that awful feeling again. Being helpless but aware of what's going on around you. I had no idea who was there. When they wheeled me out again I only saw Abella and MiaBella. The tears were flowing I was still not talking.

Here we go again. The bright lights and ice-cold room with countless people milling around. I wanted to pray but I didn't remember how. I was gone again. This time they got it right! After a few hours, I was back in my ICU room, but it looked different.

"Am I back in my room?" I asked.

"Yes, you are and everything is okay. By the way, you want some company? There are a ton of people out there for you." The nurse, a different one responded.

I saw Abella and MiaBella and the tears started. Then I saw Arlin. I cried so hard at the sight of him. No matter what we had been through, he was my rock. I can't explain that one. Then I saw my Pastor and only I would say "I must be alive... Pastor has on jeans! If I were dead he'd of had on a suit!" Everyone just laughed and said, "she's back!" I was so proud of Abella. She took care of business and made all the appropriate phone calls. I think that can go down as the worst and best day of my life.

Excuse the interruption... back to the PH diagnosis. After the surgical fiasco, Dr. Benson gave me a two-week break before going in to begin the remodulin medication. At this point I didn't care. I would do whatever he wanted. The time went quick before I had to check into ICU for the line installation and the training on how to use the medication and how to change pumps. He was correct in saying that would be the worst headache I ever had. It went well, but I had to have nurses come out to show me over and over how everything worked. That medication saved my life and carrying around a little blue pouch was not that bad.

I am currently on a few medications for PH, albuterol, aspirin, tracleer, advair, cellcept, bactrim, warfarin, remodulin. None of these medications relate to my Lupus. That's another group. I have to be absolutely med compliant. With the remodulin I have to be so compliant that I wear a pump on my body 24/7. I have to carry extra meds and the pump where ever I go. For 3 of these meds my monthly co pay is $1600. That is nearly my entire living amount. I could never afford it if it were not for grants. I am very grateful for the grants but they are not guaranteed and I have to apply every year. As I continue on in my wilderness, I am sure that God has a plan and I will live on with Him within me and I will continue to thrive.

Chapter 21

LEFT LONELY AND COPING

I am so lonely I should wear a shirt with that saying on it. I find myself just as lonely now as when I was married with a houseful of people. I have been reading my journals from my past life and they are sad. I cry as I read and it hurts still. I finally figured out the worst thing about Lupus for me is the loneliness. I'm so confused in my heart, my body and my mind. Remembering the pain of wanting my husband's touch and then getting that touch and suddenly deciding I wasn't interested. Some of the things I wrote in those journals were pretty raw and downright nasty. When I say nasty I'm talking kinky nasty. Something that could make a good romance novel. I explained often what I wanted from Arlin and what I would do for him and to him. One journal in particular, nearly half the book was duct taped and stapled close. I finally got the nerve to see what I was hiding but wouldn't throw out. While reading some details I could only wish to be in that position now, on this boring and lonely Saturday night.

I'm living in a world all alone. It used to be because I wanted it that way. Then being selfish and feeling sorry for myself I would cry out in loneliness. That feeling was not just a romantic feeling. I wanted a friend, but I pushed everyone away because I was embarrassed of who I had become while living the life of Lupus. I didn't want to be around family or go anywhere that I might run into someone I might know. I am still living that life now, but now it is mostly because I don't feel well enough to go out. The only place I am comfortable going is to the hospital. I look forward to those dates because I like talking to others and providing Lupus awareness and pulmonary hypertension awareness. I usually don't have to start the conversation because people are curious about my pump and chest bandages and I love it! But, when no one is talking I feel extremely alone. I'm wishing that someone cared enough to go to my appointments with me. Then again, I am so weird and private I don't want anyone going to the doctors with me. My mind is so tangled with all the medications, the diseases and the confusion of life. The odd thing is everything that I'm saying applies to right now and since my first diagnosis.

Since I couldn't get any attention from my husband I thought that it was time to take on a lover. I was scared to death to get involved with someone I didn't know. So, I started thinking about my past and who might be available or game for some fun. While I was still at the bank I just happened to run into and old sweetheart that dumped me just before I met Arlin. With him, I wanted to get revenge and then walk away. But, that wasn't so easy. I must have a type because he was also a cop with the same birthdate as Arlin. He lived in Wisconsin so our get togethers were planned and fun. I had someone telling me everything I wanted and needed to hear. Then I got sick again and we lost touch.

I wasn't really the type of person to sleep around, but I needed contact with someone that would gladly hold my hand, take me out to dinner and talk on the phone for hours. I found that person as well. I went to dinner with a few guys just to feel normal. When I went out I rarely spoke of my illness. When I got sick I just disappeared. I found myself talking to anyone that would talk to me. I got away with my indiscretions because Arlin was doing the same thing. He would never think I was capable of such antics. It just felt good knowing he had nothing on me. This activity was also a result of bi-polar manic kicking in when shopping wasn't enough. I did smile on those occasions. There was also still some intimacy between me and Arlin when we did get together. But in the end, I was still one sick and lonely lady.

I am naturally at a different stage in my life now. I am still a single woman and that sometimes can be lonely, but I am at peace with the life I have been dealt. I feel that lonely vibe mostly on Saturday nights. I think that's because Arlin and I always had a standing Saturday night date, no matter what was going on. I sometimes find myself wishing for a companion, but not a husband because I'm not willing to let Arlin off the alimony hook. I almost got into a serious relationship, but I realized just in time that I would be settling and I can do bad all by myself! So, here I sit proudly being the best woman I can be. On Saturday nights, I put on my soft music, turn the lights down low and take my night meds. I have a big glass of wine and drift off into my world, slowly shedding those familiar tears of loneliness and accepting the will of the universe.

Lupus kicks up so many emotions. Self-pity, anger, hurt, sadness, and often a little happiness are all mixed in there. It's so important to always be aware and stop, think and rationalize before acting on any one emotion. The medication is very capable of making one believe you got this when you really don't. You will not always be down with Lupus. It goes into remission and one can feel perfectly fine. It's important to stay in tuned with the remission. I have found many outlets for my good days and sometimes my good months. It is very easy to get caught up with feeling good and then over doing it. I feel as though I can conquer the world, then I have over worked my body and I am down for weeks. For me, that's where my loneliness kicks in.

I have learned what I can and cannot do to combat my loneliness. The biggest triumph is to not wallow in it. I tried going back to work part-time, but I soon remembered I was not very dependable. I tried volunteering, but had to admit it was kind of difficult because someone is still depending on you. Then, I reached out to the Lupus foundation because they are always looking for help. I started participating in the support groups and doing a Lupus Awareness booth at various health fairs. That works out well because they understand the illness and it is not an everyday thing. They have an annual Lupus walk for a cure as well. There are many ways to be involved and to be abreast of the latest Lupus findings. I also started speaking at different events in the intercity. I found there was a big gap in information in the African American community.

This was the most rewarding. I had suffered from so many diseases caused by Lupus and it felt good to share my story. I even started talking one on one, over the phone in an attempt to answer questions about the disease and how to live with it. Since my Pulmonary Hypertension diagnosis, I have been spending time volunteering with the PH organization spreading awareness and being involved in support groups. Another coping mechanism for loneliness was starting a blog and a Facebook page to chronicle my life with Lupus. I have recently started what I call a Beatitudes Happiness bag. I create little giveaways in a zip lock bag. I keep a supply in my car and when I come across a homeless person or a person in need, I hand them the bag. I typically target people at highway entrances or intersections. The bags usually contain hats, gloves, a snack or two and hopefully a piece of fruit and three to five dollars. Now that is a joyful feeling! When I am pulling up and they come running for change, I pass a bag of happiness. I also have a daily routine I follow to combat loneliness and the disease in general. My routine is called personal planning for my health. I look forward to sharing my purple personal planning guide.

Chapter 22

FINDING HOPE

After living with Lupus for thirty years I am still rolling with it and I am truly grateful for the journey. It has given me the opportunity to perhaps make some issues a little bit easier for someone else who's suffering from it. I wish I could've said my journey ended with my list of health issues being nearly none, but that is an unreal hope for me. It is very important to keep up with your various diagnoses. Lupus is very unpredictable and can strike upon another health issue one may have.

I thought since I've been being nothing short of real in telling my story, it would be appropriate to share where I stand with my health issues now. I am going to simply go down the list from my last hospital visit. This list is so helpful and I carry a copy with me at all times as well on my refrigerator for paramedics. I wear a pump with medication infused 24/7 and if I happened to be unconscious this list will let the EMT's know not to stop my pump for any reason. This medication is the Remodulin. I am on it for Pulmonary Hypertension. I carry a lot of information as well as a backup medical bag wherever I go. Right now, I am stable but my pulmonologist does not foresee me ever being able to come off this medication. This means I will be wearing this pump for the rest of my life.

My health issues are as follows:

Asthma, Anxiety, Aortic regurgitation, Bipolar Disorder, Cardiac Pacemaker, Cerebrovascular Accident {stroke}, Chronic Anticoagulation, Coronary Artery Disease, Dizziness, Dysarthria, Essential

Hypertension, Femoral Artery Pseudo-Aneurysm, Fibromyalgia, Hallux Valgus, Hemiplegia/Hemiparesis Late Effect Cerebrovascular Disease, Migraine Headaches, Mitral Regurgitation, Panis Disorder, PFO (Patent Foramen Ovale), Pseudo Aneurysm, Pulmonary Embolism, Pulmonary Fibrosis, Pulmonary Hypertension, Reactive Depression, Systemic Lupus Erythematosus, Systolic Dysfunction, Tinnitus, and Vertigo.

My medications are as follows:

Tylenol/Codeine #4, Albuterol Inhaler, Aspirin, Baclofen, Bisacody, Tracleer, Celexa, Klonopin, Diphenhydramine, Advair diskus Inhaler, Hydrocodone, Plaquinil, Lithium, Meclizine, Prednisone, Cellcept, Revatio, Bactrim, Remodulin, Coumadin and of course the lifesaving oxygen.

There you have it! This is my medical life and the times it has put me through. I can smile and talk about all this with ease these days because I am at peace with my circumstance. It has not been an easy road, especially when all the other circumstances of life want to jump in and play double Dutch. Again, I share this very private information in hopes that maybe someone struggling with Lupus fight may gain insight. There are many medications available to treat Lupus and pulmonary hypertension even though there currently is not a cure for either. When your doctor prescribes you a medication, research it. Doctors are not Gods. They are simply God's tools. They can and will make mistakes. Remember, this is your body and your health so you have to take care of it.

The last time I was in emergency, I found myself having to explain Pulmonary Hypertension to the doctor. I had to pull out my notes to make sure I had it right and then he left to go do more research. Trust me, I have learned to treasure my body. It's my temple and I trust it to no one but God. Be diligent in your fight. Use the internet, but never trust just one. Then verify with your doctor. For normal visits doctors schedule for fifteen minutes, so you must go in prepared. Make notes about everything going on. If you speak with them like you know your body and you are willing to take care of your body, they will give you as much time as you need.

No question is dumb. The more questions the better. Do not be embarrassed to admit you don't understand something. If you get a doctor you don't feel comfortable with, you have every right to search out another one and keep searching until you find your fit. One thing doctors despise is a patient that is not med compliant. I didn't start the healing process until I became compliant. I never miss my medications. As you can see from my list I have a lot of meds to take daily. I use a medicine tray with the days and time slots on it. I fill my tray weekly, unless I am traveling. Then I fill two trays and tape them down, so I don't have to travel with a boatload of medicine bottles.

If it is at all possible try to have all your doctors together. I have my Internal Medicine doctor and 6 specialists who all work under one roof. That's the best feeling because all the systems are linked and they can see everything about me. If you are able to get that kind of connection do it by all means. If your doctors are spread out, then it's important for you to keep track of your records. In this day and age all doctors should supply a visit summary. Keep it! The best thing is to get a folder so you can manage your care. Remember it's not up to the doctors, so don't try and leave up to them.

Lupus is a disease that you will probably find yourself fighting alone. Not because there is no love, but because it is so hard to understand. For the loved one looking in... they are at a loss of how to help, especially when you've been blessed to be able to still look like a star. All they see is the normal looking person staying in bed sometimes for days and just saying I don't feel well and I am so tired. Never give up hope with this journey. A cure is coming! Always remember all the days won't be bad. The sun will shine and when you get those days take advantage of them.

The problems of living with Lupus have been overwhelming for me personally. I sometimes can't help but think about what my life would have been like if I wasn't blessed with this mysterious illness. I am usually able to shake those thoughts off because what if's don't mean anything to me. This is just the way it is. Lupus can and most often will make your life very challenging, especially when it is active and out of remission. When it's active it becomes a awaiting game. You wait to see what part of your body will be affected this go around. As you wait there might be joint pains, extreme fatigue and confusion, which was one of my biggest problems. I would get lost while driving and have to call someone to pick me up. Depression, as I have expressed through my story, can be a nightmare especially when you recognize it. In the first stages of Lupus coming out of remission, you still look fine. Nothing is visible. Friends, family and coworkers will blast you with that awful statement, "You don't look sick..." When that happened I found myself learning to smile and not even comment. My favorite statement now days is "Thank goodness I don't look like what I've been through." I'm thinking about putting that saying on a tee shirt!

I have never ignored the limitations of my disease and because of that I was often portrayed as lazy. I did not ignore my limitations trying to impress anyone. I honestly feel that played a part in my survival. I had to plan every move I wanted to make and I am sure this played a role in my failed marriage. I couldn't keep up nor did I want to. Being very strategic in my planning got me through a lot of crises. I learned very quickly that I had to be able to explain this disease. The big problem with explanations was no two people usually have the save symptoms. I was always challenged with the statement that I know someone with Lupus and they say the same thing. I was always careful to direct my comments and explanations towards me while sharing that no two people experience the same symptoms at the same time.

Many people never experience life threatening symptoms with Lupus. Then you have a person like me that has been given the death sentence on more than five occasions. Yet, here I am. I have known a few people that the Lupus was the culprit of their life being taken away. The Lupus did not kill them but it was the underlying cause. That's because it targets the kidneys, heart and/or lungs. I am still in awe of my God because I have fought off those diseases. The only one I wasn't able to beat was the kidney disease.

As a group, we might suffer from Systemic Lupus Erythematosus, but under no circumstances can we be grouped together as far as our symptoms. Adara, my oldest child, was diagnosed one year to the date that I was diagnosed. Our symptoms were and are so different. She kind of just blew it off because she was in middle school. I remember being so jealous of her because she kept going. Her main problems with the Lupus was blood issues. She was a regular patient as well. I was left to take care of her as well as myself, but in the end we made a good team. There was a time she was home-schooled and I took that time to teach her how to run the house. If not for her, I don't know if I would have made it. I am guessing that two women in the house were sickly must have been hard on Arlin. He couldn't deal with it and for the most he is missing in action. That would be a hard pill to swallow for anyone. I know you are wondering why I didn't speak much about her and Lupus, it's because she is currently putting pen to paper as she is writing her own book. I am fully expecting her to carry on this Lupus fight even after I am gone.

Working with Lupus can be done, but it all depends on how one's body is affected. Remember Lupus is a chronic illness and is recognized by Americans with Disabilities Act. An employer cannot discriminate against a qualified person. I didn't have any problems getting what I needed from my job. Of course, that was because Lupus steamrolled through my body leaving me with kidney disease, thus getting Social Security Disability was quite easy. Again, everyone is different. I am just sharing my story in hopes that a little help can come from it.

This journey may seem like a lost cause for some, but believe me it is not! As I coped with this disease I found a circle of support. Unfortunately, that support did not come from my family, but I searched out support groups. I started with The Lupus Foundation, which is a national organization that can lead one to various support groups. They answered all my questions. I started to get involved by setting up booths at various health fairs and learned so much from that interaction. I eventually started speaking on the subject, which was where I got my confidence to live. I started smiling and realized I wasn't in this alone. No one with Lupus has to go through it alone. Smile even when you don't feel like it. You've got this!

Chapter 23

THE COUNTRY AND THE COWBOY

I've been all things for all people. My babies were all grown up and doing their own thing. I hadn't been feeling too great for a about a month or so and was still waiting on the doctor to get back to me with my most recent test results. When my phone rang, it was Doc calling to confirm that with my most recent series of health complications, things were only going to continue to go further downhill from here. That's when I decided to create a bucket list. Before I couldn't do anything at all I wanted to do everything I always dreamed of doing but never did. I sat down and began writing my list of everything I wanted to do before my final day came. It read:

Adele's Priority Bucket Checklist:

- A hot air balloon ride
- Travel around the world taking pictures
- Shooting a gun
- Go fishing Road trip
- Get in a car and drive and explore
- Go to Hawaii
- Go to a rap concert
- Stay in a resort
- Go horseback riding
- Stay on a ranch
- Get the royal spa treatment

After I wrote out my list I became more and more excited about the adventure I was about to go on. The first thing I was going to do was a road trip...just get in my car, drive, and explore the world. I grabbed my suitcase out the hall closet and began packing with the little energy I had left. I laid down and took a nap and by the time I woke up it was the next morning. I showered, dressed, grabbed my keys and hit the open road. Along the way I stopped at different souvenir shops and snapped as many pictures as I could so I could remember this trip. I had no set place and no set route. I was just rolling. It had been quite a few hours since my last stop when I saw a ranch that was having a county fair and giving away free horseback riding lessons.

It was a nice sized, country looking place called Havenwood's Bed and Breakfast Retreat. It was beautiful! It had all kinds of animals and the most beautiful horses I had ever seen. As I looked around I noticed the sign said, "Under New Ownership." In amazement at the beauty of it all, I found myself pulling in to check the place out more. Next to the sign for free horseback riding lessons stood this young, caramel colored, long haired girl brushing the mane on one of the horses. She looked to be about 17 or so. I decided to walk over and ask about the horses and the lessons. As soon as we began talking we were interrupted by the girl's father asking about a different horse. While he was approaching us, his scent danced across my nose taking me back to my house party days. It was too familiar to me. I stood there reminiscing, deep in thought when I heard "daddy this lady was asking about the horses and the lessons." I turned around and when we locked eyes he was grinning from ear to ear.

"You don't recognize me?" He spoke excitedly.

"Should I?"

"Yea you should! Parker High, McKinley Park, Skate Co.... The Kissing Rock" He started listing different things to jolt my memory.

"OH, MY GOOOODDDD... Oh my GOD... Oh my GOD!!! Ricardo Havenwood! My first true love! You've changed so much."

I screamed as I realized who he was.

"Where have you been? What happened to you? What are you doing with yourself these days? It's been too long!"

"Well I just retired from living up north in MN. I came down here to Waco, TX and bought this bed and breakfast. That's my story in a nut shell. But we have so much catching up to do. How long will you be staying here?"

"Actually, I'm not staying at all. I was just passing through and saw the free horseback lessons. I thought I'd get a lesson in so I can check it off my bucket list."

"Your bucket list?"

"Yes, you see I have Lupus..." I began explaining my condition. I told him about my bucket list and why I was traveling.

"I'm sorry to hear that. Can you at least stay for a while so we can get caught up with one another? I can also help you check items off on your list." I think he was really just volunteering so he could spend as much time with me as possible.

"Sure, I'll stay for a while." Since I had no set destination I was good with staying.

He escorted me into his bed and breakfast, offered to give me some private horseback lessons later on in the evening and showed me to my room. On the way to the room he gave me a small tour of the facility. My eyes lit up when I saw the pool area, which included a hot tub and sauna. I couldn't wait to go in there. Once I settled in and changed clothes I headed back downstairs to relax in the hot tub. I was even more thrilled when I walked in and no one was in there but me.

I slid into the water as the steam from the hot tub fogged the door and windows to the pool area. Soaking and relaxing I drifted deep into thoughts of Ricardo in our younger days. He was the boy that made my heart skip a beat at the sound of his voice. I reminisced on all the laughs and conversations we shared. I was so consumed with my thoughts that I hadn't realized how much time had passed until I became startled by the door swinging open and a firm voice yelling "THE POOLS CLOSING IN 10 MINUTES!" The deep feeling of not wanting to leave the soft warm bubbling waters surrounded me, soothing my stressed body to end. It must have been written all over my face. As I stood to exit, the firm voice began to turn in my direction. It was him!!! He looked into my face, and said

"Well... we meet again, huh?"

"I guess so." I stated softly. "... though it would be hard not to with me staying at your Ranch."

"You look like you're not ready to go."

"I'm not..." I said with a big sigh. Now I'm not sure if it was the lighting in this area or what, but I was starting to see Ricardo as I did when we were younger. It was puppy love to the max!

"You can stay in the hot tub on one condition... you allow me to join you after I lock up. I'll finish wrapping everything up around here and we can catch up with each other and enjoy one another's company."

"Hurry back" I bashfully agreed to the terms. I could feel the smile spreading across my face. My cheeks were becoming hot. I closed my eyes and laid back in the calming waters awaiting his company.

Ricardo quickly returned to join me in the relaxing steamy water. After what seemed to be a brief conversation the jets went off. When we looked up at the time we realized it was very late. We were looking like prunes together.

"Are you up for more bubbles?" He asked this with this smirk on his face.

At that very moment, I found myself blushing like a teen all over again. Sitting and reminiscing about old times brought back so many memories. Yet when he asked about bubbles, I got such a rush of adrenaline and simply said "well... we do have unfinished business."

Before he could blink I grabbed him and planted a kiss so deep my breaths danced in his soul... I abruptly stopped and apologized, but before I could say another word I was being pinned up against the pool walls. This is something I would never do, but I threw all fears and insecurities about myself out the window to embrace this moment. Hell, that's what this abrupt trip was about for me! So, I gave it my all. My eyes filled with feelings of acceptance as he tried to fight the enormous urge to scream. I was actually embracing the take charge in Ricardo. He intrigued the inner depths of the exotic nature within me. Cries rang out all over the pool room like a principal with the morning news and lunch menu.

I continued to have chills up and down my spine as replays of what just happened danced in my head while I walked back to my room. Ricardo went back to making rounds across the property, but I had a feeling I would bump into him again before I checked out to continue my trip. The emotions running through me had me almost forget to call in and at least check in on my children. I needed to do that even though I knew they didn't care as long as I wasn't in their hair. During my stay at the ranch checked almost everything off my bucket list. I had such a great time I ended up staying at the ranch for a week until Arc, the Midwest rapper called wanting me to meet him in Hawaii. He was doing a concert there, wanted company and was paying for my airfare and hotel accommodations. I packed up and set sail!

Chapter 24

THE FINAL FAREWELL

Twelve hours later I landed in Kapolei, Hawaii. I was utterly exhausted but I still felt a rush of excitement as I captured pictures of the most gorgeous places I had ever seen. A driver was waiting for me as I exited the airport and took me to the Keanma Luxury Spa & Resort. I was greeted by women and men with lays to go around our neck and drinks! It was a sophisticated urban scene in a marina community. I walked in my room, sat my bags down, stripped, showered and laid across the bed, wrapped in a towel. Between the traveling and the ups and downs of my emotions a sista' was tired! I laid there taking deep breaths, enjoying my first moment of silence in what felt like forever. Beyond excited to be on the one place I dreamed about the most. I began drifting off. Startled by the ring of my phone, I let out a deep sigh while reaching over to grab it. It was Arc! I mean Carter. An instant rush of flutters inside quickly consumed me. I got myself together and softly answered the phone.

"Why hello there, how are you?"

"Hello, my divine lady of the hour. I have a surprise for you... get dressed! I'm sending a car to pick you up. See you in a few."

Silence followed the call ended alert from my phone. I was puzzled and looked down at my phone to see if the call had really ended. Yes, it did! Should I get up? Should I call back? I mean what a minute... without thinking another thought I called his phone back... voicemail... Then a text comes through, *your car will be arriving in approximately 45 minutes!* Was he serious?

As I sat up and ran my fingers through my hair, I was actually intrigued by his take charge manner. Just the thought of how spontaneous this was gave me such a burst of energy! I was revived and without a second thought I quickly dressed, fixed my hair and headed to the lobby to await for my ride.

"Are you Adele ma'am?" I looked to see a handsomely sharp dressed man in a black and white 3-piece suit.

"Yes, I am"

"This way ma'am"

I followed him around the corner to a black shiny SUV. Now I was watching the street lights dance as I rode silently. In one way, I felt so exclusive and another a little nervous due to not knowing where this driver was instructed to take me. But, I'm here now... so what the hell! I only live once!

We pulled up to a music hall and I could hear the concert from the street. As we came to a stop, Arc was standing there waiting. He opened my door and said, "hello beautiful, are you ready to go on this adventure with me?" I slightly nodded my head and reached for his hand and was greeted by his other hand with a bouquet of my favorite flowers. Orchid lilies! They were absolutely stunning! We went to the top of the building to a private banquet hall filled with more lilies. As I blushed at the sight of all the flowers and the setup, we were greeted by the waitress with my favorite wine.

After dinner, we headed downstairs and walked through a private entrance. On the other side of the door was a hall. We followed a corridor that lead me to the side of the stage in the music hall. They were having a major music festival and Carter was headlining the festival! How awesome is that! I couldn't contain my joy at all this. I had to pinch myself to see if it was real! Ouch! Yes, it's really happening! My kids would freak out! Ha! Mama still got it! He looked at me, smiled, then pulled me on stage to be with him. We danced the night away. I was having the time of my life. The concert ended about 1 a.m. and the next show wasn't until 11 so we headed up to our rooms so I could rest a little before show time.

Being on stage at a concert like that was amazing! The lights were flashing everywhere, the beach was filled with fans tailgating and awaiting his performance, then seeing how he rocked the crowd was mesmerizing! Everyone on the beach in Hawaii was screaming his name, including me! It was so mind blowing. Even I completely let loose to enjoy the concert. Singing the songs, being entertained and the music blaring from the speakers had my body moving! "ARC! ARC! ARC! ARC!"... is all I could hear. I looked out into the crowd with the beautiful background of a burnt orange, purplish sunset with gentle winds blowing. You could see the joy in my smile. The rushing feelings of serenity and happiness were irreplaceable. After getting back to the hotel Arc guided me to the penthouse.

"This isn't my room" I stated.

"It is now!" Grinning from ear to ear I proceeded to go into the room.

He led me to the bathroom and suggested I get comfortable. In the bathroom was a hot bubble bath with rose petals floating on top. He stripped me down and helped me step inside. He stripped down and joined me. We washed each other then sat with our arms around each other just talking and relaxing. After about an hour Carter excused himself and got out. I laid there a few more minutes than exited myself. I dried off then began to wrap the towel around me when I noticed the most plush robe, slippers and fashionable lounge wear laid out on the counter with a note that read For you my love! I dressed and went to find him. The slippers felt like I was walking on clouds.

I stood against the wall watching him as he stared out the balcony window, deep in thought. How awesome is he! I said to myself. He looked up from the window to notice the gaze in my eyes at him.

"Are you ok?" he asked. I was still running on excitement.

"Actually, I've become a little hungry and could use a light snack."

"Well we can take care of that."

He sent a text then there was a knock at the door. A waitress brought in a fruit and vegetable platter, sat it on the table and walked away. That's when my alert went off on my phone. "OOOH NO! I completely forgot it was med day" I said under my breath not knowing he heard me. I was startled when he walked up and escorted me to sit down and eat and take my meds. As I ate he asked all kinds of questions about the meds and the process for taking them. As I got comfortable I started explaining all the steps with him by my side. I didn't realize until now that he was the first to be interested in me and my meds. He wasn't nervous nor afraid. Finishing up my med changes, the waitress returned with a push cart and what smelled like a feast fit only for a king and queen! Oh, we ate and sipped wine and laughed for what seemed like forever.

In the middle of a hearty laugh he pulled me to him and began to kiss me gently. He looked me in my eyes and told me I have such a beautiful soul that he just wanted to explore and nurture it! I was in awe! I was in Hawaii in a luxurious penthouse suite. I just attended the most epic music festival concert where I was the guest of the headliner of the concert. I've had nothing but his full, undivided attention and enjoying every minute of it with the soft breeze from the balcony brushing across my rosy cheeks. Before I could blink my lips were being caressed in way that made me weak.

As we were nearing our best note yet he stopped! Yes, stopped! Stopped to look in my eyes filled with passion to say, "I love you and as my queen I will provide all your heart desires." I responded with a whisper in his ear as I pulled him closer "you already have and I love you too." I laid there for a while before I was able to regain the feeling in my legs. I watched as he drifted off into what I call the best sleep ever. I noticed the sun peaking over the ocean view as my eyes began to close. Startled by the knock on the door he felt me jump, pulled me close and whispered "don't worry baby... I got you." It was the waitress saying breakfast is on the patio. I laid my head back down, closed my eyes and stared at him until my eyes could stay open no more.

About an hour or two later I was awake again. I felt sick and disoriented. I didn't want the moment to end but I needed to move quickly. My heart racing, palms sweaty, and pains ripping through my body like a hurricane in the ocean. I looked at him and decided to let him sleep for a minute while I gathered myself. I slid from under parts of his body, freshened, robed myself and stepped out onto the beautiful patio that lead to the beach. I couldn't put my figure on it but something wasn't right. These feelings seemed familiar yet more intense. Hoping it would pass since I was so far away from my doctors I took a seat at the table. Where fresh rose petals were sprinkled throughout an incredible spread of fresh fruits, bagels with crème cheeses, muffins and freshly squeezed orange juice with chilled champagne for mimosas. I nibbled a little thinking maybe it would help but it didn't. The dolphins played on the horizon of the gorgeous waters as the sun rising.

When he realized I was gone he came looking for me. He said he felt me missing in his sleep. The emotions behind what I was feeling eventually began to show on my face. My body was crying out for some rest but to me it felt like my body was giving up right when I needed it the most. We moved over to the couch. I laid my head on his chest and we talked more about everything under the sun until it was time for him to head over to a press conference and sound check. I was thinking about this incredible man and wishing it would last forever. I was actually able to relax. As he was leaving he kissed me so softly and passionately that I almost lost it.

"I'll be back before you know it" He said.

"Goodbye" I replied as tears began falling from my eyes.

Struggling, I made my way back to the table, grabbing the notepad and pen on my way. I picked up a glass of champagne and began write.

Dear Carter,

Meeting you was by far the greatest thing that's ever happened to me. I wish we could have shared more time but these past couple of days with you has been magical. Everything I never thought I could have and everything I've always yearned for you've given me. You've made me the happiest woman this side of heaven has ever seen. I wish we could've spent a lifetime together but my body isn't going to allow us to be great but my heart is with you. Don't be sad baby. I love you beyond the moon and back. I'll be waiting on the other side for us to be together again. Until then reach for the stars and achieve greatness. This is the number for my daughter Adara 414-222-3456. Send my body back to her and she'll know what to do from there.

Luv's up,

Adele

I sat back in my chair with my legs crossed as the sun beat down on my face, listening to the dolphins jump around. A peace I've never felt consumed me. Enjoying the moment, I laid my head back, closed my eyes and drifted away... still smiling at what was.

In Memory In Memory of Gina Elizabeth

This book was created in memory of Gina Elizabeth. She was a loving mother of three. She joyfully entered this world on September 1, 1958. During her life, Gina took a job in banking and diligently worked her way up the corporate later, ultimately becoming assistant Vice President of Operations at First Wisconsin Bank (now known as US Bank). She remained there until her body could no longer function in its once vibrant capacity. She was diagnosed with Systemic Lupus Erythematosus. Completely disrupting her career, she was forced to take a medical retirement as she courageously battled her illness until she peacefully departed on January 15, 2017.

During the strongest moments of her battle she became an

advocate for the Lupus Foundation. She thoroughly enjoyed the time she spent with them, encouraging other warriors fighting for their life. She wanted to express to others how difficult her journey was, but that no matter the difficulty of the road traveled anything can be overcome. Whether a warrior or supporter, it is important to understand not to get focused on one set plan. Be able to adjust to the plans changing if need be as they sometimes do. Learn the importance of respecting the needs of the body and learning how not to sink into a depression. However, if you do, understand that you can't stay there. You have to climb out when it happens. She wanted people to know how she survived with a therapist and not be afraid to be open for help.

Where ever she went she shared her story and her message. She touched lives worldwide and encouraged everyone to live to their fullest potential. Gina Elizabeth was a God sent angel who blessed the world with her presence and left imprints in the hearts of everyone she came across until it was time for her to return home.

Letters to Mom

Mommy,

We spent a lifetime talking about life's possibilities, all that we would do and become together. Every day I will awaken with the light of your spirit shining through me. There aren't enough words to express how much I miss you. In your final moments, I made a promise to you and I'm living it out. I am going to carry your legacy on into the future. I will make sure the world knows your story about your struggle with Lupus.

Luv's Up,

Ti amo Mommy

Dear Mama,

YOU ARE LOVED!

I didn't tell you this often enough, but I love YOU. You were such an important person in my life and I most definitely appreciate all that you've done for us. Thank you for all of the sacrifices you made. Please know that nothing you've done has gone unnoticed. I was in denial that you were as sick as you truly were and figured that

you would pull through like you always did. I wish I had more time with you. All that I am or hope to be in life, I owe to......
MY ANGEL!

Terrance Eliuah

Mommy,

Words can't describe how much I love and miss you. You have taught me so many things and I am doing my best to make a difference and be the best person I can be. You are and always will be the most beautiful, strongest, and most influential person I've ever known and I will never forget the lessons you taught me. I know this book meant everything to you and it's finally complete! I hope it makes you proud. You can rest now my dear, I love you.

Love,

Jaymii Alea

Plan to Live

Be anxious for nothing, but in everything by
prayer and supplication, with thanksgiving let
your requests be made known to God.

Philippians 4:6

The purpose of this section is to provide you with helpful tips and strategies I learned along the way that can help you cope with your battle with chronic illness. My goal is to guide others living with chronic illness with the task planning their lives daily so it works for them. Make sure you are precise in your answers because that's what it will take for each individual to come up with their plan and be free to adjust it based on their mind and body.

- Don't be embarrassed to let people know you don't feel good
    - o Ex: You could pass out and people don't know what's wrong and it may make the situation worse
- Healthy eating habits are very important
- Meditation helps a lot
- Don't be one tract minded about your treatment plan. Be willing to try new stuff 136
- Build a relationship with your doctor and tell the truth. Don't say you're not feeling something if you are because it may go untreated.
- Research the diagnosis and medications they tell you
- Journal Daily as another outlet to release and express your feelings
- Create a vision board so you can envision where you see

your life. It can help you focus and manifest your visions into a reality. It's a great start to help you begin putting your life back together when you feel like it's falling apart.

- Think about doing yoga because it will help you relax and help you find your peace
- Create a medical cheat sheet for your supporters to make them better prepared to be able to assist you in case of an emergency

o Full Name	o Allergies
o Date of Birth	o Medications, Dosage
o All Diagnoses	Amount, Number of
o Blood Type	times taken
o Closest contacts you	o Pharmacy
would like called in	o Doctors names, contact
case of an emergency	numbers, and clinics
and their numbers	o Insurance Carrier
	o Home Address

Laminate it so they can carry it around and act immediately if needed.

- Create a POA (Power of Attorney) over your medical. Someone you trust to make sound medical decisions on your behalf if you're not able to.

Plan Out Your Daily Routine

It is very important to schedule out your daily routine and maintain it. When setting up your guide it can be grouped into morning and night time routines, different categories, or outlined 137 like below. Columns can be simply stated as am ritual and pm ritual. Choose whatever method you are most comfortable with. The guide below is just one of many examples. When setting up your daily routine it's important to know nothing is too small.

DATE:

AM	Today I must do	Today I must contact	Today I must go to	Meals & Meds
12:				
1:				
2:				
3:				
4:				
5:				
6:				
7:				
8:				
9:				
10:				
11:				

PM	Today I must do	Today I must contact	Today I must go to	Meals & Meds
12:				
1:				
2:				
3:				
4:				
5:				
6:				
7:				
8:				
9:				
10:				
11:				

In Case of Emergency Notify

Keep an ICE (In Case of Emergency) contact in your phone or on you at all times. Make sure you have their name, address, and phone number so that if something happens to you the people helping you will know who to contact.

Name: _________________________________

Address: _________________________________

Home Phone: _________________________________

Cell Phone: _________________________________

Work Phone: _________________________________

Relationship: _________________________________

Medical History

Keep a list of all your medications, diagnosis, symptoms, and blood type so that if you pass out or something people know what's wrong, the medical staff will know what to do, and if a blood transfusion is needed they will know what type of blood to use.

Name: _________________________________

Date of Birth: _________________________________

Blood Type: _________________________________

Preferred Hospital: _________________________________

Allergies: _________________________________

Primary Doctor: _______________________________

Chronic Conditions:

1. _______________________________

2. _______________________________

3. _______________________________

4. _______________________________

5. _______________________________

6. _______________________________

7. _______________________________

8. _______________________________

9. _______________________________

Current Symptoms:

1. _______________________________

2. _______________________________

3. _______________________________

4. _______________________________

5. _______________________________

6. _______________________________

7. _______________________________

8. _______________________________

9. _______________________________

10. _______________________________

Notes to The Doctor:

____

____

____

____

____

____

____

____

My Medications

Medications:	Dosage:	Frequency:
1. ______________	______________	____________
2. ______________	______________	____________
3. ______________	______________	____________
4. ______________	______________	____________
5. ______________	______________	____________
6. ______________	______________	____________
7. ______________	______________	____________
8. ______________	______________	____________
9. ______________	______________	____________
10. ______________	______________	____________

Purpose: **Possible Side Effects:**

1. _______________________   _______________________

2. _______________________   _______________________

3. _______________________   _______________________

4. _______________________   _______________________

5. _______________________   _______________________

6. _______________________   _______________________

7. _______________________   _______________________

8. _______________________   _______________________

9. _______________________   _______________________

10. _______________________   _______________________

References

Arthritis Foundation. (2002) *Lupus.* Atlanta, GA.: Authors Arthritis Foundation and American College of Rheumatology

Arthritis Foundation. (2017). *What is Lupus?.* Retrieved from http://www.arthritis.org/about-arthritis/types/lupus/what-is-lupus.php

Arthritis Foundation. (2017). *Lupus Causes.* Retrieved from http://www.arthritis.org/about-arthritis/types/ lupus/ causes.php

Lupus Foundation of America. (2017). *Common Symptoms of Lupus.* Retrieved from http://www.resources.lupus.org/ entry/common-symptoms?utm_source=lupusorg&utm_ medium=answersFAQ

ADELE OHANZEE BIJOUR